He had deliberately ruined her lovely day!

Celine didn't know whom she hated most, Nicky or his cousin Oliver.

As Oliver drove her away from the theater she exploded, "You knew Nicky and his wife would be there, didn't you?" She stopped because she was going to cry — the last thing she wanted to do, especially in front of Oliver.

"Yes, I knew," he replied imperturbably.

"I don't want to go out to supper with you, now or ever — I don't want to see you ever again!" She added fiercely, "Nicky said you always interfered...."

"Tell me something," asked Oliver, "did you intend seeing Nicky again? Willingly?"

"Of course not!"

"You are in fact crying for the moon. Far more sense if you looked up at your star — your midsummer star, remember?"

BETTY NEELS
is also the author of these
Harlequin Romances

Many of these books are available at your local bookseller.

For a free catalog listing all titles currently available,
send your name and address to:

HARLEQUIN READER SERVICE
1440 South Priest Drive, Tempe, AZ 85281
Canadian address: Stratford, Ontario N5A 6W2

Midsummer Star

Betty Neels

Harlequin Books

TORONTO • NEW YORK • LONDON
AMSTERDAM • PARIS • SYDNEY • HAMBURG
STOCKHOLM • ATHENS • TOKYO • MILAN

Original hardcover edition published in 1983
by Mills & Boon Limited

ISBN 0-373-02566-1

Harlequin Romance first edition August 1983

CHAPTER ONE

THE May sun, bright but still tepid so early in the morning, shone down on the old house, so that the rose brickwork and the tilted gables glowed; it shone on the Albertine roses, already in bud, climbing its walls, and on the large neglected garden around it. And it shone too on the girl, idling to and fro on the swing under the great mulberry tree on the edge of the lawn at one side of the house.

She was a big girl, splendidly built, with a lovely face framed by dark curling hair, her creamy skin already faintly tanned by the spring sunshine. She was wearing beautifully cut slacks which had seen better days and a silk shirt with its sleeves rolled up above her elbows. That was well worn too but of excellent cut. She swung slowly to and fro, her dark brows drawn together in a frown, for once unaware of her beautiful surroundings. She said softly: 'Something will have to be done.' And the elderly Labrador lying beside the swing cocked an ear and turned mild brown eyes to look at her.

The girl put up a shapely hand to push the hair away from her face. She looked around her, at the herbaceous border on the far side of a lawn which badly needed mowing, the hedge of lavender, the paved path leading to a half hidden pond, and beyond to the tumbledown fence and the fields. She sighed and allowed her gaze to dwell on the house, quite enchanting in the sunshine; a small

Elizabethan manor house, a jewel of a place to
the casual eye, but to those who lived in it a
constant source of anxiety, with its leaky roof,
woodworm in the beams, damp seeping up into
the passages and old-fashioned kitchen. Nothing,
she reflected bitterly, that couldn't be put right
with money. Only there wasn't any of that; her
father, absentminded scholar that he was, had
drawn steadily on his capital for years now, and
her mother, her dear, charming mother, hadn't
economised; she had tried, with the best will in the
world, but she had no idea how to set about it,
and if Celine suggested that they should have a
casserole instead of roast pheasant or salmon
trout, her parent always had a ready answer, even
if an illogical one.

Celine got off the swing, strolled back to the
house, opened the door in the kitchen garden
wall and went through to see how things were
growing. Thomas, the very old gardener, did very
little now, but he was still paid his full wages, it
would never have entered anyone's head to have
done otherwise, but they badly needed help. Celine
did her best, but she was still the veriest amateur.
The expensive boarding school she had been to
and the finishing school in Switzerland hadn't
taught gardening, and when she came home, it was
taken for granted that she would stay there, doing
the flowers, playing tennis with numerous friends
in the neighbourhood, helping with the annual
Garden Party and the Church whist drives, and
going occasionally to London with her mother to
buy clothes. Expensive clothes too, Jaeger and the
better class boutiques, and Raynes or Gucci for
shoes. And she hadn't given it a thought; her

father had lived all his life in the old house, and his father and grandfather before him, and heaven knows how many forebears. So she had rather taken it for granted that there was money enough. When occasionally she had mentioned the leaky roof and the peeling paint, her father had looked vaguely surprised for a moment and had remarked that he really must do something about them. But he never had; she realised with a shock of surprise that she had been home for three years; it was only during the last few months that she had begun to notice things. Old Barney was still with them, but then he had been her father's batman during the war, and Angela, their cook, who had always been there too. But when Joan the maid had left to get married, she had been replaced by Mrs Stokes from the village who obliged twice a week, and several bedrooms had been shut up.

She bent and pulled a couple of radishes, rubbed the earth off them, and crunched into them. She should have done something about it, of course, and she felt bitterly ashamed. Here she was, twenty-two years old, nicely up in the social graces but a complete stranger to shorthand and typing, nursing, teaching the young, or even serving in a shop, and without any of these skills how was she to get money, because money was what was needed; her home had to be kept from falling to the ground. It was a pity that she had refused the wholesale manufacturer of cotton goods who had wanted to marry her; he was a rich man. Indeed, now she came to think about it, she had refused several comfortably off young men, under the impression—mistaken, she now saw—that one should marry for love.

She whistled to Dusty, stretched out on the grass path, and turned back to the house. Mr Timms, the family solicitor, was coming to see her father that morning; her mother had mentioned it and looked worried, but when Celine had asked what was the matter, she wasn't told anything. That was the trouble, she thought unhappily; she had been born unexpectedly when her parents were verging on middle age, and they still thought of her as a child to be shielded from anything unpleasant. Not that they had spoiled her, but she had been brought up in a kind of effortless comfort; money was never mentioned and she hadn't bothered over-much about it. She loved her home dearly. If she hadn't perhaps she would have trained for something and got a job by now . . .

She went in through the kitchen door, stopped to talk to Angela, whose elderly feet were hurting her, then went through the stone-flagged passage to the hall; there were flagstones here, too, and panelled walls and oak rafters and narrow latticed windows. She stopped to smell the lilac standing in a great vase in one corner and went into the dining room.

Her mother and father were already there, her mother, a small, pretty woman with bright blue eyes, busy with her post, her father, tall and thin and scholarly, behind his newspaper. Celine kissed them in turn and took her seat at the table.

'What time is Mr Timms coming?' she asked. Her father didn't answer; she turned her lovely grey eyes on her mother, who looked up briefly.

'About ten o'clock, dear. We'd better have him to lunch.'

Celine poured herself some coffee and began on

a boiled egg. 'Father, why is he coming?' And when her parent grunted: 'Is it about money? I've never bothered about it, I'm afraid, but now I think I ought to be told.'

He lowered the paper and looked at her over the top. 'There's no need . . .' he began.

She interrupted him gently. 'There is, you know. Father, are we broke?'

He looked uneasy. 'The truth is, my dear, I'm not quite sure. It is true there isn't a great deal of money left, and unfortunately I made one or two investments a couple of months ago and they haven't turned out quite as I had hoped.'

She buttered some toast. Her insides were cold, she could hardly get the next question out for very fright. 'We shan't have to leave here . . .?'

'Unthinkable,' declared her father. 'In any case, who would buy the place? It's falling down.'

'But Father, isn't there anything to be done? I mean, couldn't we patch it up a bit where it needs it most?'

Colonel Baylis was on the whole a mild, rather dreamy man, but he could, on occasion, return to the parade-ground manner. 'There's no need for you to concern yourself about such things,' he told her severely. 'We shall come about; Mr Timms will advise me . . .' He retired behind his newspaper once more and Celine turned to her mother.

'Mother——' she began.

'Your father is always right, darling,' said Mrs Baylis, and Celine sighed and went on eating her egg. Her mother was a darling, but she was impractical, she had no idea how to be economical, and it was a little too late in life to begin now. She wondered what Mr Timms would have to say.

Whatever Mr Timms had to say was for her father's ears alone, it seemed. The two gentlemen retired to the Colonel's study as soon as he had arrived and didn't emerge until it was almost time to have lunch, when they joined Mrs Baylis and Celine in the drawing room; low-ceilinged, panelled walls, and shabby but still grand furniture. They drank their sherry and made polite conversation, then they crossed the hall to the dining room, equally low-ceilinged but a good deal smaller, its chintz curtains faded to the pale pastel colours of the Savonnerie carpet, its dark oak furniture adequately dusted but unpolished.

The lunch was excellent; Angela was a good cook, and Celine, who had learned to cook to Cordon Bleu standard at the finishing school, had whipped up a delicate soufflé to follow the pâté and toast, with a fruit tart to follow. But however excellent the fare, it did nothing to dispel Mr Timms's severe gloom; even the Chablis the Colonel had fetched from the cellar hadn't helped. Celine, taking her part in the talk, bided her time.

She had her opportunity presently, when after a decent interval drinking coffee, Mr Timms prepared to leave. He had taken the village taxi from the station, but now Celine said quickly: 'I'll run you down in the car, Mr Timms,' and was on her way to the garage before anyone could object.

There were two cars—a far from new but beautifully kept Jaguar and a Mini. The Jag soaked up petrol, but somehow she couldn't see Mr Timms squashed into the Mini. She drove the big car round to the front of the house, where she found him waiting outside the open door with her parents.

As she turned out of the gates at the bottom of the short drive she asked: 'Will you tell me what it's all about, Mr Timms? And I'm not just being curious; Father has hinted . . . it's so hard on them both. They can't change their ways now, you know, but perhaps there's something to be done.'

'I don't know . . .' began Mr Timms primly, then looked astonished as Celine stopped the car on the side of the lane. 'If you tell me quickly,' she said sweetly, 'you'll be in nice time for your train.'

'This is quite improper——' he began testily as she turned to look at him. She was a lovely girl, her enormous eyes beseeched him. For once he stifled his professional feelings. 'The truth of the matter is,' he began, 'your father has almost no capital left—a thousand or so, and barely enough from the rents of his property in the village and the farms to cover his rates and taxes. He invested against my advice, a good deal of money over the last few years, with disastrous results.' He paused and asked anxiously: 'Should we not be driving to the station?'

Celine started the car and went slowly ahead. 'Go on, Mr Timms,' she begged.

'The house is in a woeful state of repair—even if your father were to put it on the market I doubt if anyone would buy it, and then at a sum far below its value . . .'

'We can't leave,' declared Celine, and despite all her efforts her voice shook a little. 'It's been home for generations. Has Father any income at all?'

'Over and above the rents—they will take care of taxes and so forth—he has a small income of—let me see—about fifteen hundred pounds a year.'

Celine gulped. Her father had given her mother

a mink coat at Christmas; it had cost a little more than that. 'If I could think of a way to earn some money, how much do I need to get by? I don't think we can count on Father's income . . .'

The station was in sight and she heard Mr Timms's sigh of relief. 'Just to live,' he stated, 'food and fuel and the servants' wages and the very minimum of upkeep, at least seventy-five pounds a week, and that would be cheese-paring indeed. You do of course grow your own vegetables and fruit, do you not, and you have hens? . . .'

'And plenty of wood for fires, only they make a lot of work. But work is what I'll have to do, isn't it, Mr Timms?' Celine smiled at him and he found himself smiling back at her, wondering why such a lovely girl hadn't found herself a rich husband. Rich or not, he'd be a lucky man.

'Thanks for telling me,' said Celine, and bent forward and kissed his cheek.

'There's really nothing you can do,' he assured her.

She looked at him with bright eyes. 'I've been doing nothing for a long time,' she told him gently. 'I think I'll try something else for a change.'

She didn't hurry back but dawdled along the lanes pursuing impossible schemes for making money in a hurry and abandoning them in turn. It was as she passed the last cottage on the very edge of the village that her eye caught the Bed and Breakfast sign Mrs Ham was hanging in her front window. It was like watching sudden fireworks or opening a door on to something breathtaking as the thought struck her. She accelerated and swept through the open sagging gate. 'If Mrs Ham can, so can I,' said Celine loudly.

She put the car away and went in search of her parents, whom she found sitting in the drawing room, her mother bent over her tapestry, her father standing with his back to the French window with Dusty beside him.

They both looked at her as she went in, but before either of them had a chance to speak she began cheerfully: 'It's all right, I prised it all out of Mr Timms—and don't be angry, Father, I have every right to know. Most girls like me are pinning down good jobs and paying their own way, but I've just been living here and costing you money—now it's my turn. I think I know a way in which we can go on living here, even if we do have to cut down a bit.' She studied their upraised faces and thought how elderly and tired they looked and how much she loved them. 'Bed and breakfast,' she announced, 'and evening meal if anyone wants it. No taxes to pay, cash coming in to keep us ticking over. Mr Timms says the rents will cover taxes and rates and so on; we can cut out the electric fires and we don't need the central heating until the autumn, and there's plenty of hot water from the Aga. We could at least give it a try, and I'm just spoiling for something to do.'

She waited for them to reply, and it was her mother who spoke first. 'Darling, it's a lovely idea, but it's impossible—there are ten bedrooms and it's a big house and so difficult to run—there's only Angela . . .'

'And me, Mother, and you.' And at Mrs Baylis's startled look, 'Oh, not housework, darling, but if you did the flowers and laid the tables and ordered the food——'

'And what should I do?' enquired her father.

'Well, Father darling, you could see to the wine—there's plenty of that in the cellar, isn't there? You can sell it . . . and stroll around making sure everyone's happy and write out the bills.' Celine smiled at him. 'Do let's give it a try. It needn't cost much to get started; we'll need a week to get the house ready and open up the rooms and get out the linen and silver. Please, Father, we've nothing to lose.'

'We'll need help . . .'

'Not at first. We've got Mrs Stokes and Barney and we might only get a handful of people and we could cope with them; the moment we've a little money to spare we can get a girl from the village.'

'We might get no one at all,' said her mother.

'Well, we aren't losing anything, are we? I mean, we live here anyway, don't we, and so do Angela and Barney, and we already have to pay them.'

Her father left the window and sat down at the sofa table, where he took out his pen and an old envelope from his pocket. 'I wonder how much cash we should need to get started?' he mused out loud.

There was a great deal to do. Half way through the week Celine found herself wondering if she would ever have suggested it if she had had even an inkling of what was involved. It wasn't just opening up the rooms, airing them, polishing the furniture and making up the beds. There were bedside lamps to find and bulbs to fit into them, soap and towels, the casement windows to oil because most of them squeaked abominably, the three bathrooms, all old-fashioned, to pretty up.

And then downstairs—she had never realised what an awkward house it was to keep clean. She had dusted and Hoovered from time to time and done the flowers and polished the silver, but these tasks had never been allowed to interfere with visits to friends and trips to town. Now Celine found herself caught up in a routine of hard work, so that she fell into her bed at night quite worn out. But she discovered that she was enjoying it. The old furniture gleamed with polish, the silver, brought out of its felt bags, was made to shine, glasses which hadn't been used since the last dinner party at Christmas were brought from the butler's pantry. And in between all this, Celine found time to draw up lists of groceries with her mother, make up a few hopeful menus, and retire to the big shed at the bottom of the kitchen garden and paint a large sign. This she nailed to a tree by the gate, aided by old Thomas who strongly approved of the whole idea. 'All them broad beans and the rhubarb and I don't know 'ow many raspberries coming along a treat, there'll be more than enough for 'em.'

Colonel Baylis ignored the sign and went back into his study with the new batch of books from Hatchett's, but his wife wandered down to the gate and admired it in her gentle way. 'Very nice, dear,' had been her comment. 'I hope someone comes today.'

But no one did. The next day passed, and the next. The Colonel said nothing, he ate his meals almost in silence and then went back to his books, and Mrs Baylis said hopefully: 'Well, it was a splendid idea, darling, I'm sure someone will come soon.'

'They'd better,' observed Celine darkly, and went outside, where she relieved her feelings by painting a gutter she had managed to heave back into its rightful place. She was perched half way up the ladder when the car came up the drive, and when it stopped and two elderly ladies got out, she came down pretty smartly and went towards them.

Retired schoolteachers, she thought, taking in the sensible skirts and blouses and cardigans, and said good afternoon politely.

The older and taller of the ladies addressed her with faint hesitation. 'You do bed and breakfast?' she asked. 'We're looking for somewhere quiet and not expensive.'

'It's very quiet,' said Celine, trying not to sound eager. 'We charge six pounds for bed and breakfast and if you would like to have dinner, that's three pounds fifty.'

The ladies exchanged a glance. 'If we might see the rooms? We should require two rooms, of course.'

'Do come in,' invited Celine, and just stopped herself from dancing through the hall and up the stairs.

She showed them the two nicest single rooms there were, at the back of the house, and as luck would have it, one of the bathrooms was just across the passage.

'No washbasins,' commented the younger of the two ladies.

'It's a very old house,' said Celine. 'Tudor, you know, and modernising it has been very difficult. But this bathroom will be for your sole use.'

'We'll take the rooms, and we should like dinner. Do you have a varied menu?'

'Hors d'oeuvres, local trout, vegetables from the garden, egg custards and cream or rhubarb tart and cream. Chicken supreme if you would like that, but it would take a little longer. We have a good cellar too.'

She smiled at them both. 'I'll fetch your bags,' she told them. 'Would you like tea? Just tea and sandwiches and cakes, fifty pence,' she added.

'That would be nice.' The older of the pair joined her. 'I'll get our cases from the trunk and perhaps you'll tell me where to put the car.'

Barney was crossing the hall as they went downstairs, and Celine gave a silent chuckle; he gave just the right touch to the house and she knew that her companion was impressed. She called softly: 'Barney, would you be good enough to take these ladies' cases to the back wing? And then go and ask Angela to make tea for two?'

She showed the lady where to put the car in the vast covered barn beside the garage and ran back to the house. Her mother was in her own small sitting room, writing letters.

'Mother, we've two guests—tea and dinner as well. Shall I put them in the small drawing room?'

'Darling, how marvellous! Yes. Shall I go along presently? Does your father know?'

'Not yet. Will you tell him? I'm going to the kitchen to help Angela.'

It was really rather fun, Celine decided as she got ready for bed that night. The ladies had eaten their tea, served on a silver tray and with paper-thin china, in the smaller drawing room, not much used because it was so damp in winter, but very impressive with its painted panelled walls and Regency furniture. And they had dined equally

splendidly in the dining room at the back of the
house which Celine had set out with several small
tables, nicely laid with linen damask that had
been stored away for years. She had waited at
table herself and had enjoyed it all, although now
she was in bed, she felt tired. But who cared about
being tired, she told herself, when there would be
twenty pounds in the household purse in the
morning.

The Misses Phipps left soon after breakfast,
making for Wales. 'If we'd known that this part of
Dorset was so charming we might have stayed,'
they explained. 'We've always driven straight
through before, along the main roads, but pure
chance brought us here.'

'And let's hope that pure chance brings a few
more this way,' said Celine, standing beside her
mother outside the door. 'I'll just get the beds
made up and then get the washing machine on the
go. Do you think Barney could get the fire laid in
the sitting room? Just in case . . .'

She smiled at her mother, dropped a kiss on her
cheek, and ran indoors.

It was after tea when two cars turned into the
drive. They stopped untidily and the man behind
the wheel of the first car got out. Celine had seen
them from her bedroom window and reached the
open door just as he came in.

He was a large, cheerful type and his, 'Hullo,
love,' was hearty. 'Can you do bed and breakfast
for six? And what's the damage if we stay? Two
kids, mind. We'll want three rooms.' He eyed
Celine, very pretty in a deceptively simple jersey
dress which had cost far too much the previous
summer. 'You the lady of the house?'

'No, the daughter. Yes, we have rooms for you. We charge six pounds each for bed and breakfast, and if you wish, you can have dinner here—that's three pounds fifty.'

He looked doubtful and her heart sank. 'Proper rooms?' he wanted to know. 'We paid twelve pounds at the hotel last night and a tenner for dinner.'

'We aren't a hotel. But the rooms are—are quite proper and our cook is excellent. Perhaps you would like to see a room before you decide?'

Celine led the way upstairs, past the family bedrooms and those with the fourposters and the lovely views, and showed him three rooms in the east wing, all charming, although she very much doubted if he would appreciate them.

'Old house, isn't it, love?' he enquired. 'Can't see any washbasins.'

'It's Tudor, and we don't have washbasins, I'm afraid, but there is a bathroom here.' She opened a door and let him look in.

'Looks all right,' he said. 'O.K., we'll sleep the night. And have a meal—we're pretty peckish— How long will we have to wait?'

'Less than an hour. If you would like to settle in and then come downstairs...'

'No chance of a beer, I suppose?'

'I'll ask my Father to fetch some up. Lager or ale?'

'A pint of mild and bitter'll suit me, Grandpa the same, I daresay—the ladies will want a drop of port, I daresay.'

They went downstairs again and Celine pulled the embroidered bell rope by the front door for Barney—'Some luggage to take up to the east wing, please, Barney'—and he followed her out to the cars. There were several small cases; she hoped they would tip him, she must remember to ask him.

They were a noisy lot and the children, eight or nine years old, were whining that they wanted ices. Sharp slaps from their mother, a high-complexioned young woman in tight jeans, stopped them whining and started them crying instead. Grandpa and Grandma, bringing up the rear, had little to say, only stared around. Celine left them thankfully and shut the doors on them all while she went to find her mother and father.

'I've put them in those rooms in the east wing,' she explained. 'They look—well, I wouldn't like them to damage anything . . .'

'Should we use the silver?' asked Mrs Baylis.

'If they're paying what we ask, they're entitled to the best treatment,' pronounced the Colonel sternly.

But it was hard to give the best treatment to people who didn't really mind if they got it or not. They ate a delicious dinner and pronounced it nice enough, but regretted loudly that there were no chips. They also commented upon the dreary paintings on the walls, and long-dead Baylises stared back at them haughtily. They wanted sauce with almost everything they ate and spilt things on the tablecloths. All the same, Celine rather liked them. They would have been much happier at Mrs Ham's down the lane, for to them, the house was just a tumbledown place, too dark and furnished with out-of-date stuff they didn't fancy. She made a point of asking them what they would like for breakfast and got up very early to cycle down to the village to get the cornflakes they fancied and the kipper fillets Grandma hankered after.

They ate a huge breakfast, and now that it was a bright morning and the house was alight with sunshine, they were more at ease. 'Haunted, are you?' asked Grandpa.

Celine shook her head. 'No—everyone who's lived here has been happy, you see.'

'Pity for a pretty girl like you to be stuck in the country,' he observed.

Celine smiled at him. 'Ah, but I'm a country girl,' she told him.

It took a little time to get them away. Barney, looking every inch the English butler, carried down the luggage, helped stow it and received a tip with dignity. Celine was tipped too; she detected uncertainty in the man's manner as he pushed it into her hand, so her smile was charming as she thanked him. 'That's very kind of you,' she said. 'I hope you all enjoyed your short stay.'

'Not 'arf,' said Grandpa. 'It's a sight better than Butlins.'

The two cars disappeared through the gate, and Celine went to the sitting room where her mother was counting money.

'My dear!' she exclaimed, looking quite excited. 'Fifty-seven pounds—and all for nothing, as it were!'

Celine didn't correct her. There was the little matter of four beds to strip and make up, three rooms to clean and the dining room to put in order.

'It's a good start, darling. Let's have coffee. Do go and tell Father and I'll go to the kitchen.'

Barney met her with a grin. 'A pound, Miss Celine—not bad, eh?'

'Super, Barney. Angela, they gave me a pound for the cook.' She handed over her own tip and made her way upstairs.

It was a lovely day. By lunchtime everything was just as it should be once more, and the three of them had their meal on the covered verandah at the side of the house, and afterwards Celine wandered into the garden and sat down under the mulberry tree. She was half asleep where she sat when she heard a car coming up the lane, she was strolling towards the front door when a Rover turned in at the gate.

There were three people in it, but only the driver got out. Celine stood still, her lovely mouth very slightly open, her breath stilled. Here was the man she had always dreamed about, tall, dark, handsome in the best tradition of romance and smiling at her as though she was the answer to his dreams too.

'Hullo,' he said. 'You look like a fairytale princess. We saw your notice at the gate—any chance of putting the three of us up for a few days?'

A few days! She couldn't believe it: all these years, waiting for him, and here he was. She smiled and looked so breathtakingly beautiful that he blinked.

'Yes, of course. How many—how many rooms would you need?'

'One for my parents, one for me. Come and meet them.' He put a hand on her arm. 'The name is Seymour—Nicky. What's yours?'

'Celine Baylis.' She stole a glance at him and found him smiling.

'What a lovely name—it suits you.'

His parents had got out of the car and were looking round them, the man elderly, upright and grey-haired, his wife almost as tall, very slim and well dressed. The best bedrooms, Celine decided as they shook hands.

They were delighted with their rooms and the tea which Celine served in the garden under the trees. She longed to stay and talk to Nicky Seymour, but her mother had asked her to make a special effort with dinner. 'They might stay a few days if they like the food,' she said, 'and they seem such nice people—your father and Mr Seymour seem to have a lot in common.' She added: 'I like his wife too, and their son seems a nice young man.' She sat quietly for a moment. 'That's almost thirty pounds a night, and they've had tea and I heard him asking about wines with their dinner.' She beamed at Celine. 'I put a bowl of anemones in their room.'

Celine bent and kissed her mother's still pretty cheek. 'You're a wizard with flowers,' she told her, and sped to the kitchen where she and Angela between them conjured up homemade soup, trout with almonds, lamb cutlets with spinach from the garden and a rhubarb crumble with cream. It was after they had eaten these that Mr Seymour declared himself willing to remain for at least three days, especially as the Colonel had offered him a rod on the stretch of river running through his fields.

'And I shall just sit,' declared his wife. As for Nicky, he said nothing, but he had smiled at Celine in a way to make her heart beat very fast indeed.

The next two days passed delightfully. Mrs

Baylis was happy, doing little sums on the backs of envelopes, the Colonel was happy because he had congenial guests who appreciated the wines he had to offer them, Mr and Mrs Seymour were content to relax and Celine and Nicky spent a good deal of time together; every moment that she could spare, in fact. The mornings were busy enough, what with beds to make and rooms to tidy, but lunch was cold and salads took no time to make, so that after she had served their meal, cleared away and had hers with her mother and father, there was a good deal of the afternoon left. Her one secret dread had been that other people might arrive and want rooms too, but this didn't happen, so she was free to stroll in the gardens or walk down to the village with Nicky, who proved to be a delightful companion and a very attentive one; the world had suddenly become a splendid place in which to live and the future full of vague but delightful promise.

It was on the third day, as they strolled back from a walk beside the stream, that Nicky caught her by the arm and turned her round to face him.

'I can't believe my luck,' he told her, 'finding you here. I didn't know there were girls like you left in the world. We shall be going in a day or two, we've a family to visit in Wales, but when we get home, you're coming to stay with me.'

Celine was too honest to pretend that she wasn't delighted. 'Oh, Nicky, that would be super! Don't you work, though? What do you do?'

He kissed her before he answered. 'Oh, I'm learning to step into Father's shoes, I suppose.' He shrugged his shoulders. 'Working in London is boring, but of course we spend a good deal of time in Berkshire.' He smiled at her. 'London will be fun if you're there—we'll dine and dance and go to a few shows . . .'

She drew a little way away from him. 'It sounds heavenly, but I couldn't possibly come until the autumn—we might be very busy until then.'

He said carelessly: 'Can't you leave that to someone else? Hire someone from the village?'

'No. I started it, you see, so I must see it through, but no one comes this way once the summer's over.'

He shrugged impatiently. 'Oh, well, we'll have to see, won't we?' He sounded so offhand that she had a mind to say that she would go to London just whenever he wanted her to, indeed her mouth was open to utter the words when she heard her mother calling her, and something urgent in the sound of it sent her flying up to the house.

They were all in the hall; Colonel and Mrs Baylis, Barney, Angela Mrs Seymour and Mr Seymour, who was lying on the floor unconscious.

'Celine . . .' begged her mother in a wispy voice. Celine knelt down beside the elderly man and took a good look. He was breathing, but in a heavy stertorous way and he made no response to her urgent voice.

'Barney, telephone Dr Grady—ask him to come at once. Mother, turn back the bed in the dressing room by Mrs Seymour's room. We've got to get him upstairs.'

She looked around her and her father nodded. 'Right—but we'll need more help . . .'

Nicky had been standing well back, but now he came forward and said reluctantly: 'You'll need a hand. What's the matter with him?'

Celine was too anxious to do more than feel momentary surprise at his words, but perhaps he was so shocked . . . They picked Mr Seymour up carefully, the three of them, and got him upstairs and on to the bed. Celine took off his shoes and covered him with a blanket and undid his tie. 'We'd better not do anything else until Dr Grady comes. I'll stay here with him, if you like, Mother. I'm sure Mrs Seymour would like a cup of tea . . .'

She had expected Nicky to stay too, but he didn't, so she found herself alone with the quiet figure on the bed, trying to think sensibly. Would Mr Seymour go to hospital—and the nearest one was at Dorchester, quite a way away—or would he have to stay where he was, in which case it wouldn't be practical to have anyone else in the house. She went to bed and stood looking down at the nice elderly face, flushed now and somehow one-sided. As she looked, the lids lifted and the faded blue eyes stared back at her. She bent down and caught one of his hands in hers. 'Mr Seymour, it's all right. You're in bed, the doctor is coming . . .'

He tried to speak and she bent lower to hear him. After several attempts he whispered thickly: 'Oliver—send for Oliver.'

She murmured soothingly. Who in the world was Oliver?

The hand in hers stirred urgently. 'Oliver . . .' He was lapsing into unconsciousness again and remained so until Dr Grady came into the room.

'Good girl,' he said softly. 'Stay here, will you? In case—In case I need anything—his wife is too upset. Has he roused?'

'Yes, he managed to say something. Send for

Oliver—I expect Mrs Seymour will know who that is.'

'We can ask presently.' He began his examination and presently straightened. 'A stroke, but not too severe. A week's rest—he'll have to stay here. I'll get hold of a nurse, then as soon as he's fit enough he can go home by ambulance.' He grinned at her. 'I'm being hopeful, mind you.'

'Yes, well, that's all right, we'll manage. I suppose we'd better not have any other people while he's here? I mean, bed and breakfast people.'

'I heard about that in the village. Well, there's no reason why you shouldn't. Heaven knows the place is large enough to swallow a dozen just as long as they're not too noisy. Extra work for you, though.'

There was a movement at the door and Nicky came in. He said shortly: 'Well, what's the damage?'

Dr Grady glanced at him with shrewd eyes. 'A slight stroke; nothing too worrying, I hope, a week's rest should make it possible for your father to return home. He'll need a nurse, I'll see about that. Celine tells me he was asking for someone . . .'

'He wants me to send for Oliver.'

Nicky frowned. 'Oh, good old Oliver, everyone's mainstay and prop,' and at her enquiring look: 'My cousin—he's a doctor, worthy and dull. I suppose if Father wants him he'll have to be sent for.'

'I'll stay here while you telephone,' said Celine, 'and would you ask Barney to come up and we'll get your father into bed.'

'O.K., I suppose we'd better send for him. Let's hope he can tear himself away from his precious patients.'

He went out of the room, leaving Celine vaguely unhappy.

'Not much love lost there, presumably,' said Dr Grady, and watched the ready colour creep into her cheeks.

'He's upset,' she said softly, she didn't meet his eyes. 'Perhaps this cousin's what he says—he sounds tiresome.'

CHAPTER TWO

DR GRADY came back that evening, bringing Nurse Stevens with him—a severe, stout lady, bordering on middle age, but reluctantly, if tinted hair and elaborate make-up were anything to go by. Celine relinquished her patient thankfully, showed Nurse Stevens to her room and offered a meal. 'If you'll just say when you would like your meals, I'll come and sit with Mr Seymour,' she offered. 'Did you have to come far?'

'Yeovil. I've told Dr Grady that he must find a nurse to do night duty; I'm prepared to sit with the patient tonight, but I can't work all day and all night too.'

'No, of course not. I'm sure he'll get someone to share your duties. Until then, I'll help all I can, and I'm sure Mrs Seymour will sit with him to give you a break.'

Nurse Stevens spoke bitingly. 'I'll decide for myself, thank you, Miss Baylis. In the meanwhile, perhaps I could have something on a tray later on—about nine o'clock will do. And something left out for the night, of course.' She cast a disapproving eye on the faded wallpaper. 'You have servants, I suppose?'

'Two. But this is a difficult house to run; I'll look after you, Nurse Stevens.'

Celine made her escape and met Dr Grady coming out of the drawing-room, where he had been talking to Mrs Seymour. 'What in heaven's name have you brought us?' she demanded in a fierce soft voice. 'She wants trays of food and wanted to know if we had servants. I didn't know there were people like her left!'

He grinned at her. 'All I could get at short notice. But if it makes you feel better, Mrs Seymour is quite prepared to sit with him for as long as needed, and Oliver is on his way.'

'And if he's anything like Nurse Stevens I shall crown him,' said Celine crossly.

She was perched on the kitchen steps, slapping paint on to a worn out drainpipe when she heard the car coming. 'If that's Oliver,' she muttered, 'let him ring the bell—Barney can let him in.' She had had a rotten morning after a short night, what with carrying up trays and answering frequent bells from the sickroom—besides, she had seen almost nothing of Nicky. It had been a relief when Mrs Seymour pronounced herself quite capable of sitting with her still unconscious husband while Nurse Stevens took some exercise, which left Celine free for an hour before seeing to the tea. She hadn't bothered to pretty herself up, indeed, she had got on an old pair of jeans, paint-stained and none too clean, and a cotton sweater which had once been expensive, but now was a much washed pale blue. All the same, she looked quite beautiful on her stepladder, and the man who got out of the Aston Martin paused to look at her before strolling across the gravel towards her.

'If you ring the bell, Barney will let you in,' said Celine tartly, and added: 'Good afternoon.' She glanced down at him and saw that he was a large man, with wide shoulders and rugged good looks. His hair was fair going grey at the temples, and his eyes were very bright blue.

He looked up at her and smiled slowly. 'Miss Celine Baylis, the daughter of the house,' he observed placidly. 'How do you do? I'm Oliver Seymour.'

Celine dipped her brush in the paint. It was a pity that she couldn't quite reach the end of the drainpipe, but she went busily over a bit she'd already done till he reached up and took the brush from her. 'If you'll come down, I'll just do that end bit for you.'

And she found herself doing just that, standing ungraciously while he finished her work, put the brush tidily in the jamjar on top of the steps and the lid on the paint. 'Could we go into the house?' he suggested gently, just as though she should have suggested that minutes earlier.

Worse than Nurse Stevens! she decided silently, marching him briskly towards the front door; he was going to be one of those infuriating people who took charge the moment they poked their noses into anything.

She flung the door wide. 'Do come in,' she said haughtily. 'Mrs Seymour's sitting with Mr Seymour—the nurse is taking some exercise, but I'll find Nicky.'

His eyes searched her face. 'Ah, yes, Nicky—of course.'

He had a pleasant voice, deep and rather slow, but something in its tone made her glance at him. He returned the look with a gentle smile.

Lazy, she thought, and a bit dim—knows everything better than anyone else but can't be bothered. Why on earth is he here?

She left him in the sitting-room and went in search of Nicky, whom she found asleep in the drawing-room. The look of irritability on his face when she wakened him rather took her aback, but it was replaced so quickly by a charming smile that she imagined that she had fancied it.

'Your cousin has just arrived,' she told him, and was disconcerted to hear the deep voice just behind her.

'Ah, Nick—a pity to have disturbed you. I'll go straight up to Uncle James, if I may, and see the nurse later. Is Aunt Mary there too?'

Nicky had sat up, but not got off the sofa. He stared up at the big man, leaning against a chair with his hands in his pockets. 'As far as I know,' he said ungraciously. 'It's all such a nuisance . . .' He caught Celine's surprised look and went on smoothly: 'It's been a terrible shock.'

'I can see that,' said his cousin, his voice very even. He turned on his heel and Celine perforce followed him out of the room; she would rather have stayed with Nick, but someone had to show this tiresome man where his uncle was.

Half way up the stairs he asked: 'I see you do bed and breakfast. Have you a bed for me?'

She said stiffly: 'There is a room, yes. Have you come far?'

'Edinburgh.'

Celine opened the bedroom door and went quietly into the room. Mrs Seymour looked up from where she was sitting by the bed. The delight and relief on her face as her nephew crossed the room towards her was obvious.

'Oliver—oh, now everything will be all right! He's been asking for you. Dr Grady is coming later this afternoon, you will be able to talk to him.' She smiled at Celine, standing quietly by the door. 'I don't know what we would have done if it hadn't been for this dear child.'

'There's a nurse?'

'Yes, she's out walking.' Mrs Seymour pulled a face. 'Very serious and severe and rather a trial to the household, I should imagine.' She smiled from a pale face. 'Perhaps you could use some of your charm?'

'It doesn't always work,' he observed, and glanced at Celine as he spoke.

She ignored the look. 'I'll bring you a tray of tea up here,' she offered, and whisked away, down the stairs, for some reason feeling peevish.

She later took tea, tiny sandwiches and the fruit cake Angela had just baked upstairs and arranged the tray on a table near the window before going to find her mother and father in the study. They looked up as she went in and her mother said: 'I heard a car, darling—but we can't take anyone, I suppose?'

'It's the nephew, Oliver Seymour. He wants to spend the night. I'll get the small room across the landing ready for him. I'd better go to the kitchen and tell Angela there'll be one more for dinner this evening.'

Mrs Baylis's eyes brightened. 'Really, darling, one wouldn't want to be unkind, but we're making money, aren't we?'

'On paper, yes. I don't suppose Mrs Seymour will think of the bill at the moment.'

'No, of course not, but Nicky might. Are we getting low in ready cash?'

'We're O.K. for a bit, darling. Would you make one of your salads for dinner this evening? I'll get a couple of lettuces and some radishes, and there'll be a few spring onions ... I'll get some apples from the loft, too.'

The Colonel looked up from his book. 'What are we eating tonight?'

'Lamb chops, and I'll make a syllabub.'

'You look very untidy,' observed her father, but she didn't have to answer him, for he was once more deep in his book.

Her mother cast an eye over her. 'Yes, love, you do. I'll see about tea and you go and change.' She added: 'Is he nice?'

'O.K., but I'll get the radishes first. I've no idea, I hardly spoke to him.'

Celine went out of the side door into the kitchen garden, her basket on her arm, and filled it with things for the salad; she was grubbing up the last of the radishes when slow firm feet trod the path behind her.

'Very soothing,' declared the deep lazy voice, 'gently pottering in the garden—good for the nerves too. Why isn't Nick helping you?'

Celine straightened her back. 'I didn't ask him to,' she said politely.

'Did he need to be asked?' His voice held a friendly mockery that annoyed her.

'He is on holiday,' she pointed out sharply.

He didn't answer that but went on placidly: 'You must have been put to a great deal of trouble with my uncle ill in the house, as well as losing customers. I'm sure my aunt hasn't remembered to pay the bill—will you let me have it and we'll settle up?'

Celine arranged the radishes in a neat row, not looking at him. 'You're leaving—all of you? I didn't think Mr Seymour . . .'

'Don't be silly,' he sounded avuncular, 'of course we aren't leaving, but we're preventing you from having a house full, and the least we can do is pay our way.' He took a radish from the basket and ate it. 'Do you do the accounts as well?'

'No, my father sees to that.' She started back towards the house. 'I've one or two jobs to do . . .'

He let her go without protest. 'Of course. Do you mind if I look round the garden until Dr Grady gets here?'

'Of course not.'

Celine had to admit, as she helped Angela in the kitchen and then went to lay the table, that he was considerate and kind. But Nick didn't like him; she wondered why. And where was Nicky anyway? They had hardly seen each other all day. As if in answer to her thought he came into the dining room and threw an arm round her shoulders. 'Beautiful girl, isn't it about time you spared a thought for me? I might have known that once Oliver got here he'd spoil everything.'

She set the knives and forks just so, very conscious of his arm. 'I've been around,' she said, a shade breathless, 'and your cousin hasn't spoilt anything. Why should he? Your mother was very glad to see him—because he's a doctor, I expect.'

She didn't see Nick's quick frown. 'Oh, I daresay. Here, drop that lot of plates and come into the garden for a few minutes.'

She laughed, feeling suddenly happy. 'I can't—look, dinner's in an hour, and I've heaps to do and I'll have to go and change.'

'Never mind that.' Nicky took the plates from her, then tucked an arm through hers and walked her through the French window out into the garden.

'It's heavenly now.' He smiled down at her, holding her close. 'I had no idea when I came on holiday that I was going to meet the only girl in the world for me.'

Celine didn't answer him, and he didn't seem to expect it, but strolled round the side of the house towards the high wall of the kitchen garden, still warm from the afternoon's sun. They were well away from the house when he stopped and put his arms round her. 'You're everything a man wants,' he told her. 'You and I are going to be very happy.'

Celine stirred in his arms. She felt shy and excited, but over and above these she felt as though she were being rushed along too fast. Nicky was going to kiss her and she wasn't quite sure that she wanted him to, not just yet. All the same, she felt a keen exasperation when the old wooden door into the kitchen garden creaked open and Oliver strolled through, not twenty yards away.

He closed the door carefully behind him and beamed at them. 'Hullo there, enjoying a little peace and quiet together?' and instead of going off to the house, he strolled towards them. Without quite knowing how it had happened, Celine found his vast person between them, a hand on their shoulders, propelling them gently forward while he carried on a gentle conversation. She answered mechanically, but Nicky didn't say a word—not then, at any rate, but when she left them in the hall, she heard him break into furious speech before she had closed the kitchen door.

Nurse Stevens came back presently, was served her dinner and went away to the sickroom, and Celine cleared away, put the finishing touches to the tables and went back to the kitchen. It wasn't quite time for dinner and everything was ready. She slid upstairs, showered, changed into a little Italian dress she had bought the previous summer, did her hair and face with the speed of light and was downstairs again with five minutes to spare. She could hear Mrs Seymour, Nick and his cousin in the smaller sitting-room; her mother and father were there too and there was no reason why she shouldn't join them. Instead she went to the kitchen again, picked up the tray with the avocado pears with shrimp sauce and took them along to the dining-room, where she met Barney, dealing with the wine. In the twilight, just with candles glowing, the shabby room looked rather lovely, and Barney, very neat in his black alpaca jacket, certainly added tone to the place. Celine wondered if they were charging enough for dinner as she crossed the hall and banged the gong.

There was no getting away from the fact that Oliver was now very much in charge of the party. Nick hadn't bothered over-much about his mother's lack of appetite, but his cousin, with a

placid firmness which would have been hard to
resist, made sure that she ate at least something of
the meal. And he saw that her glass was kept filled
too. Mrs Seymour had brightened visibly by the
end of the meal, although it was only too apparent
that Nick was sulking.

The poor boy, thought Celine, handing the salad
from the garden to go with the lamb chops, the
wretched man has taken over completely. Pompous
ass, she added to herself for good measure.

She carried the coffee into the drawing-room
when they had finished their meal and Mrs
Seymour patted the sofa beside her and said: 'Do
sit down, my dear—you lead such a busy life,
surely you can rest for a few minutes.'

'I'm not tired,' declared Celine, and meant it.
She sat down, with a quick look at the clock; five
minutes, ten at the most. She caught Oliver's eye
and coloured faintly; he saw so obviously exactly
what she had been thinking. Indeed, she waited for
him to make some remark, but he didn't, just sat
there, listening to Mrs Seymour talking about her
husband's illness. 'Of course, everything is all right
now Oliver's here,' she said quite happily. 'He's
such a splendid doctor, and he and Dr Grady
quite agree as to the treatment. And they say he's
responding to—to . . .' She looked at her nephew,
who said calmly, 'Stimuli—pins and lights and so
forth.'

Mrs Seymour nodded in agreement. 'Yes, that's
it. I was telling your mother, Celine, that just as
soon as it's safe to move my husband, we'll do so.
I feel very badly about you turning away other
guests.'

Celine said cheerfully: 'Oh, it's not quite the

tourist season yet, you know, we didn't expect to be full for another few weeks.' She paused in thought. 'And now Oliver's here too, you might be able to have one or two drives round the country.'

'Now he's here,' said Nick suddenly, 'I'm going to take some time off myself—it's not been much of a holiday so far.'

His mother looked at him doubtfully. She doted on him, but even she must have realised that he had contributed very little to ease a difficult situation, but his cousin answered readily enough. 'Why not? I'm at everyone's service.'

'Well, I hope this lovely weather holds for you,' said Celine, and got up. Oliver got up too and went to open the door for her. She thanked him coolly, not looking at him. He hadn't said anything at all, but somehow he had made poor Nick look—well, uncaring. And he wasn't that, after all, he had come on this holiday with his parents when he might have gone off somewhere exciting on his own. She was so very glad that he hadn't.

She ate her own dinner in a rosy haze of vague dreams, so that her mother had to tell her twice that Dr Seymour had paid the bill and had had a chat with her father too. 'Such a nice man,' said Mrs Baylis with the faintest of question marks in her voice, 'don't you think so, dear?'

Celine muttered something, and her father, who hadn't been listening said: 'He's an Oxford man, I thought he might be. Took his degrees at Edinburgh, been to Vienna too—quite a good man, I should suppose. A different kettle of fish from that cousin of his.'

'Nick is a very nice person,' said Celine, quite

fiercely for her, and got up to change the plates, missing the warning glance her mother shot across the table at her father. When she sat down again her mother said: 'Now we've got some money I wondered if you'd take the car tomorrow and go down to Dorchester market. I'll tidy the rooms and make the beds if you could manage to clear the tables after breakfast—you could be back for lunch. If we had something cold—I'll make a salad...'

It would be nice to have an hour or two away from the house, although she would be away from Nicky too ... 'Shall we make a list before we go to bed? Dr Seymour seems to think his uncle may be fit to move by ambulance in a week, perhaps less, and we want to be ready for the next lot.'

'Where do they live?' asked Celine, and tried not to sound eager. It was something Nick hadn't told her and she hadn't asked.

'Oh, Harrow, or is it Highgate? I believe Dr Seymour lives in London too, but I'm not sure where.'

He could live on the top of Mount Everest for all Celine cared. She didn't like him, she told herself as she helped Angela clear away for the night, and at the same time was aware that this wasn't quite true. He had done nothing deliberately unkind, he hadn't been boastful, he had been friendly and polite, and if it hadn't been for Nicky telling her what a tiresome man he was, she might even have liked him. She finished in the kitchen, said goodnight to Angela and Barney and crossed the hall to the sitting-room to say goodnight to her parents. Nicky came out of the drawing room at the same time, and they met halfway, and stopped.

He put an arm round her and smiled so that her heart turned over.

'I was hoping I'd see you. Any chance of coming for a drive tomorrow?'

'I'm going to Dorchester market directly after breakfast, and I have to be back for lunch.' Her soft mouth curved into a smile.

'Heaven-sent! I'll drive you in my car. We can't make it the whole day, I suppose?'

Celine shook her head. 'Impossible—it really is. But it would be lovely.' Her eyes shone and he put the other arm round her.

'You beautiful girl,' he said softly, and then stiffened and let his arms drop as someone, not too far away, started whistling. It could only be Oliver. It was, sauntering down the stairs with his hands in his pockets. He nodded casually at them as he crossed the hall and went out into the garden, but the magic moment had passed. Celine said in a brittle voice: 'I shall be leaving about nine o'clock.'

'I'll be waiting.' Nicky took her hand and gave it a gentle squeeze, but that was all. Any moment Oliver might appear again—like the genie in a pantomime, she thought peevishly.

She was up very early and had breakfasted long before anyone came into the dining-room. She served the meal, saw to Nurse Stevens' wants, cleared the table, fetched her shopping list and was on the doorstep by nine o'clock. Nicky was there waiting in the car, and there was, thank heaven, no sign of his cousin. Celine got in beside him with a thrill of excitement, a little dampened by his careless: 'We don't need to shop, do we? Can't you ring up for whatever you need when we get back?

It's such a glorious day, we could go for a run—
have a picnic . . .'

'Oh, but I can't, honestly. Angela wants most of
the things today—the village shop doesn't have a
great deal, you know. Besides, I must be back
before lunch—there's no one else to serve it.'

'What about that butler of yours? Or your
mother?' Nicky spoke carelessly.

'Barney's got heaps of jobs to do—not just
being a butler—he's the handyman too and he
does the vegetables and does quite a lot of
housework when no one is about. And mother
wouldn't know where to start.' She added,
suddenly fierce: 'Why should she? She's never been
used to it, and it was my idea in the first place.'

He patted her knee. 'O.K., don't get so worked
up! It was only a suggestion. But remember, when
you do get a few hours to yourself keep them for me.'

He was an amusing companion, and it was
impossible to be vexed by him for more than a few
moments. The drive to Dorchester was a delight
for her, and when they had parked the car, he took
her to Napper's Mite for coffee, and they walked
through the crowded market while Celine bought
fruit and meat, and, that done, led him into the
town to Parson's grocer's shop to buy the special
tea and coffee that her mother had had for years.
It all took rather longer than she had bargained
for, and she mentioned this as they got back into
the car, only to be made sorry for doing so
presently, for Nick drove back much too fast, so
that by the time they arrived she was on edge with
suppressed nerves. All the same, she thanked him
with warmth, refused with regret his offer of another
drive that afternoon, and went off to the kitchen

to give Angela a hand with the lunch.

The doctor had been, Angela told her as they stood side by side at the vast kitchen table, Celine making a salad, Angela putting the finishing touches to the egg and mushroom flan she had taken from the oven. 'Very pleased he was, too. That nice Dr Seymour was with him. Now there is a man for you, Miss Celine—I wouldn't mind being ill if I had him to look after me.'

'Oh, pooh,' declared Celine, and tossed her lovely head. 'He's just the same as any other doctor.'

'Now there you're wrong,' declared Angela. 'But it's no good telling you that now, is it?'

Celine muttered under her breath; Angela had known her all her life and sometimes forgot that she wasn't a little girl any more. 'I'm going to sound the gong,' she told her companion, and marched into the hall.

Mrs Seymour and Nicky were halfway through their meal before Dr Seymour joined them. Beyond a brief apology to both them and Celine, he gave no reason for his tardiness. She put a plate of chilled watercress soup before him with exaggerated care and served his companions with early strawberries and cream. In the kitchen she said snappily to Angela: 'Serve that man right if I dished up his omelette now—it'd be nice and leathery by the time he's ready for it.'

'Miss Celine, I'm surprised at you—whatever next! Such a nice man, and so considerate too.'

Celine tossed her head and snorted delicately. 'Stuff and nonsense,' she said crossly.

She stayed cross for the rest of the day, for she had no time to herself at all. Several times on her way to the kitchen garden, or racing round the house, she had glimpses of Nicky stretched out on the lawn in front of the house, but there was no chance to talk to him. She served tea on the grass under the trees and took a tray up to Nurse Stevens, then went to join her parents in the sitting-room for half an hour.

Her father glanced up as she went in. 'Busy?' he asked without really wanting to know. 'I hear from Dr Seymour that Mr Seymour may be leaving us in a day or two.' He smiled at her vaguely, one finger marking the place in the book he was reading. 'Has anyone else arrived?'

'I hope not,' said Celine, wolfing bread and butter, 'I've got my hands full.'

Her mother gave her a gently reproachful glance. 'But, darling, you persuaded us to do this bed and breakfast thing—are you bored with it?'

'I haven't had time, Mother dear. I'll be much easier when we just get people for a night or so . . . I mean, there's Mr Seymour and the nurse . . . it makes it a bit busier.'

'Yes, darling, I'm sure it does. All those extra rooms I have to put flowers in. But the money is most useful.'

Her father lowered his book. 'I must say Dr Seymour is a very fair-minded man—insists on paying the full amount for his uncle even though he is only on a fluid diet and costs us almost nothing to feed.'

For some reason Celine felt annoyed. She felt despondent too; if Mr Seymour went, Nicky would go too and she wouldn't see him again. She finished her tea and took the tray back to the kitchen, and while Angela and Barney had a couple of hours off, got started on the evening's menu.

It was much later, when she was wearily clearing the last of the dishes away and tidying the kitchen for the night, that Nicky joined her.

'So this is where you hide out,' he said, and laughed as he tucked an arm in hers. 'No, put those plates down, I haven't talked to you for hours.'

'This morning . . .' she laughed up at him from a tired face. 'And I'm not on holiday!'

He bent and kissed her lightly on the cheek. 'Ah—and that's what we must put right. I have to go to Bournemouth in a couple of weeks' time— only for a few days, but we could have a couple of nights out—surely you can take a day or so off when you want to?'

Celine was puzzled. 'Well, I suppose so, but it would be awkward, Nicky—I mean, there's no one to take over—I'm not indispensable, but I am a pair of hands. And—and . . . where would I stay?'

'Oh, at the hotel, of course,' he said easily. 'I always go to the Royal Bath.' He added softly: 'We have to get to know each other, my sweet.'

'Why?'

He raised his brows and smiled slowly. 'Don't tell me you don't feel entirely the same as I do about you. Love at first sight, you know.'

She was breathless. 'Oh, yes, Nicky—I never thought it was true, but it is, isn't it? Only I can't . . .' She paused. 'Would you wait for a while, just while I get this business going, and when it's running smoothly, I could get someone to take over . . .'

'No need for a couple of days, surely?'

Celine felt her cheeks flame. 'Oh, I thought you meant getting married.'

It sounded so gauche, the kind of remark the heroine might make in a second-rate film, but that was exactly what she had thought.

The arm around her shoulders tightened reassuringly. 'My sweet, that is what I meant. Of course I'll wait—but I do think we should see as much as we can of each other until you're free.'

Celine drew a deep breath, and the small doubt lying somewhere at the bottom of her excitement disappeared. 'I'll see what I can do. When are you leaving?'

He shrugged. 'Lord knows—or at least, my interfering cousin does; when he feels like it, I suppose he'll tell us.'

'Has he always been like that?'

'Always. There's not much love lost between us, but there's no need for you to see him once he's left here. He's always wrapped up in his precious practice and some clinic or other he runs.' He threw her a sidelong glance. 'Dislikes girls, too—had some miserable affair when he was young and has no time for women, or so he says.'

'Oh—he's always been very polite . . .'

'Well, of course—doctors always are; they cultivate a kind of veneer which doesn't mean a thing. Don't let's waste time talking about him . . .'

Nicky broke off as the door opened and Nurse Stevens came in. She said without preamble: 'Dr Seymour asked me to come down and get some fresh lemonade. Will you do it, Miss Baylis?'

Celine had pulled away from Nick, her cheeks pink. There was no reason why she should feel guilty, after all, it was her home and she was doing nothing wrong. Nurse Stevens was tiresome. She said shortly: 'I'll make a jug and bring it up, Nurse.'

She noticed that Nurse Stevens looked tired and every day of her age. It was a pity, and Dr Grady couldn't get a night nurse. She asked: 'Have you had very disturbed nights?'

'Yes, they have been rather broken, but there wasn't a nurse available and Mrs Seymour isn't strong enough to stay awake at night.' She cast a look at Nick, lounging in a Windsor chair by the Aga. 'But Dr Seymour has kindly offered to stay up tonight so that I can have a proper sleep.' She pulled out one of the chairs at the table. 'I'll wait for the lemonade.'

Long before Celine had it ready, Nicky had given up and gone sulkily away, and later, when Nurse Stevens had gone too and Celine had finished tidying up the kitchen, there was no sign of him. She went to say goodnight to her parents and then tiredly to bed.

Two days later, Mr Seymour was judged recovered enough to make the journey home by ambulance, and in those two days Celine had had almost no time alone with Nicky, only on the last evening he came back into the dining-room as she was clearing the table. 'I'll have to drive Mother home,' he told her, 'but I'll be down again in a couple of days, and that's a promise. We can fix up that weekend then,' and at her questioning look: 'And make plans for the future. Our future.'

He drew her close and kissed her rather hurriedly. 'I can't stay—Oliver's making all the arrangements, of course, and he'll be looking for me, damn him. I'll see you in the morning before we leave. I'm going to miss you, darling.'

He had gone leaving her to finish her clearing up, her sadness at his going lessened by the news that he would be back so soon.

Getting the invalid away took some time, despite the fact that Nurse Stevens had been prevailed upon to accompany him in the ambulance. But finally he was stowed away and she with him, and Mrs Seymour, having delayed their departure for several minutes, searching for things she found that she already had, got in beside Nicky. Only then did he get out of the car and go back into the house, taking Celine, waiting in the porch, with him. 'I can't go without saying goodbye, Celine. Yes, I know the ambulance has gone and Mother's impatient, but no one considers me at all.' He kissed her lightly. 'That'll have to do until I see you again . . . in a couple of days, and I shall expect to have you all to myself.'

He let her go and went out to the car. He got in with a careless wave of the hand and drove off, down the drive and out of the gates.

It wasn't until then that Celine realised that the Aston Martin was still parked at the side of the house. She turned round to find Oliver standing beside her. 'Aren't you going too?' she asked.

He smiled a little at the coldness of her voice. 'Yes—I had some business to attend to with your father. Thank you—all of you, for the trouble and kindness you've taken. We must have been a sore trial to you and we're eternally grateful. You'll be glad to see the back of us.'

He gave her a level look. 'Not Nicky, of course. You'll miss him.'

She lifted her chin, and more to hearten her own

low spirits than anything else said: 'Yes, of course
I shall, but he's coming back in a day or two.'

The blue eyes went dark. 'Indeed? To stay here?'

'It's really none of your business—as a matter of
fact, he's asked me to spend a few days in
Bournemouth so that we can go out to dinner and
see something of each other.'

His face was expressionless. 'My dear girl, don't
go.' His voice was so kind that she looked at him
in astonishment.

'Why ever not? I'll be staying at a hotel ...
besides, we're going to be married.' She took a
deep breath. 'I shouldn't have told you—Mother
and Father don't know; it's all happened so
quickly, and I can't think why I told you, because
I'm certain you'll disapprove.'

He said harshly, 'Yes, I do disapprove—for the
best of reasons. Nicky is already married.'

He stalked past her without another glance,
spoke briefly to Mrs Baylis still standing in the
porch, then got into his car and drove away.

CHAPTER THREE

CELINE stood in the hall, not moving at all, the
doctor's words ringing in her ears. She didn't
believe him. Nicky had told her that his cousin
didn't like women since he himself had had an
unhappy affair. He was jealous, unable to endure
anyone else's happiness. He had sounded so
furiously angry too. Presently she walked outside
to join her mother, determined not to remember a

word of what he had told her. Nicky would be back; she would tell him, and they would laugh about it together and make plans for a delightful future.

'You're very pale, darling,' observed Mrs Baylis. 'Why not go and rest until lunchtime?' She took Celine's arm as they began to walk through the hall. 'Well, I hope all goes well with them, they were delightful people, weren't they? And that nice Oliver settled their bill with your father—really, darling, it's so nice to see money again—I might even have a new dress ... And he left something for Bennett and Barney and Angela and thanked them all. I'm sorry we shan't see him again.' She threw a sidelong glance at Celine's strained face. 'Will you miss him?'

'I didn't know him very well, Mother. Shall we have coffee and then I'll start on the rooms—you never know, we might get some people later on.'

There was a lot to do and no time to brood, but despite Celine's resolve to forget every word that Oliver had uttered, she couldn't—his deep, quiet voice sounded in her ears, just as though he were standing beside her. She made beds with fury, Hoovered and dusted and polished, as though she could polish away all trace of the Seymours—not Nicky, of course: he would come in a day or two and she would tell him all about it and they would laugh together. The thought cheered her, so that her mother remarked over their tea: 'So you had a nice rest, dear—you look better for it.'

Celine said, 'Yes, Mother,' because there was really no point in telling her there was no one but herself to get the rooms ready. Her mother was a darling but very unobservant; things got done around the big house, and she took them for granted and never asked who did them, but that was hardly her fault. For most of her life she had never had to do anything for herself and Celine considered that it would be unkind to expect her to do so now. She drank her tea, crumbled a scone, and said she would lay up the dining-room. 'I don't suppose there'll be anyone this evening,' she observed, 'but it's nice to be prepared; besides, it means we can have a quiet day tomorrow.'

She was folding Angela's perfectly ironed table napkins into fans when she heard a car. Just for a second her heart leapt; it might be Nicky ... common sense told her not to be silly and she went unhurriedly to the door.

There were three women in the porch, middle-aged but fighting against it, with platinum hair, expensively set, carefully made-up faces. and expensive clothes, very slightly too youthful for their rigidly controlled figures.

The one in the middle spoke. 'Bed and breakfast?' she asked in an ultra-refined voice. 'We took the wrong road . . .' She sounded so accusing that Celine found herself apologising for that. 'We intended spending the night in Sherborne, but we took the wrong fork,' went on the complaining voice, 'and here we are at the back of beyond!'

Celine had never thought of her home as being that before. She said briskly: 'Well, if you care to stay, we have rooms and breakfast, and we serve dinner if you should want it. Three pounds fifty extra . . .'

'And the rooms?'

'Six pounds each.' She stood aside as they trooped in. They decided on three separate rooms, which was nice because of the money although it would make extra work, and they wanted dinner. 'If you'll show us the menu we'll let you know what we'd like,' said the woman with the refined voice.

'I'm afraid there's only a small choice,' Celine pointed out, conscious that she and Angela hadn't really got down to much cooking—somehow, she hadn't expected anyone. Vegetable soup, home-made of course, or chicken liver pâté, local trout with vegetables from the garden, or chicken with lemon, and raspberry charlotte with cream.' She watched the women exchange glances and added to be on the safe side: 'Our cook makes delicious omelettes, if you wanted something light.'

They settled for the trout, the soup and sweet, and asked about drinks.

'My father deals with those,' said Celine, and went off to warn him. They looked as though they might drink Cinzano or port and lemon, and he would erupt unless she tipped him off.

The women went the next morning, and Celine was glad to see them go. They had been exacting—not quite complaining but always on the verge of it, and they had wanted late-night pots of tea, and sat far too long over their dinner so that she hadn't been able to clear the table. They had patronised Barney without tipping him and remarked to Celine, 'Do you keep a butler? What a waste of money, and he doesn't do much, does he?'

Celine hadn't answered that, almost biting her tongue out in her efforts not to say something scathing. All the same, there was another thirty pounds to swell the amount her father had locked up in the wall safe behind the picture of Great-grandmother Baylis. Celine, doing careful sums at the kitchen table, decided that they were beginning to make a profit. Another month and she would persuade her father to get in the local carpenter to repair the rotted windowsills at the back of the house. Her mind flew ahead; then the plumber and someone to mend the roof and the house to be painted. Which would cost the earth, she warned herself, but if they could achieve that by the end of the tourist season, it would have been worth it.

Her thoughts wandered presently, she wondered where Nicky was and what he was doing; busy deputising for his father, more than likely. Oliver's voice, successfully buried during a busy day, sounded in her ears. Try as she might, she was finding it difficult to forget what he had said, even though it wasn't true. She longed for Nicky to come and tell her so. She thought about him during the whole of the morning, making beds, cleaning and tidying and getting ready the dining-room once more, and she was so absentminded at lunch that her father, never one to notice things, remarked upon it. 'You're usually chattering like a magpie, my dear—a bit off colour, perhaps?'

Her voice was very bright. 'Never felt better, Father. I've been doing sums—if we go on like this we could get those windowsills mended . . .'

He looked doubtful. 'Perhaps we should wait and see what the bills are going to be first. Extra lighting and so forth, you know.'

Celine forbore from mentioning that none of them had ever been very thrifty about turning off lights which weren't needed, she didn't think that they were using much more electricity than they had always done, but she didn't argue. Her father, easygoing to a fault, could be unexpectedly obstinate at times:

'I was wondering if we couldn't take a trip to town and get some clothes?' suggested her mother.

Celine poured their coffee and handed it round. 'Should we wait just a little longer?' she said at length. It was going to be hopeless—no, nothing was hopeless, she told herself bracingly, but it was going to be uphill work, getting her father to use the money on the right things. She added: 'You've got that lovely grey silk you bought last autumn—it suits you beautifully, why not get some wear out of it and get something at the beginning of the autumn when all the new clothes will be in the shops?'

Her mother, bless her, was easily led. 'That's a good idea, I'd quite forgotten that dress. But what about you, dear?' She frowned. 'I must say you don't wear anything very pretty . . .'

'Well, I can't during the day, but if no one comes this evening, I'll dress up tomorrow. I thought I'd pick some peas this afternoon. They're early this year, and a good thing too.'

'Your father's taking me in to the hairdresser—do you want anything from Dorchester, darling?'

Celine remembered the morning she had spent there with Nicky—she had been so happy... She said dreamily: 'No, thanks, Mother. Will you be back for tea?'

'Probably. Don't do too much, Celine, there's no need, what with Angela and Barney around.'

Angela, slaving in the kitchen and her corns fit to kill her, and Barney with his carefully concealed arthritis. Celine said calmly: 'No, Mother, of course not,' and the moment the Jaguar had gone out of the gate went to the kitchen, sent Barney and Angela off for a quiet afternoon, and finished the washing up. It didn't take long, and all the afternoon stretched before her unendingly. She was just about to go into the garden with her basket when the telephone rang. She had lifted the receiver almost before it had stopped ringing. It would be Nicky...

It was Mrs Seymour, apologetic for not ringing sooner. 'But there was so much to see to when we got home, I don't know what I would have done if it hadn't been for Oliver.'

Who wanted to know about Oliver, always doing the right thing? Celine longed to ask about Nicky, but instead enquired about his father.

'He's to see a specialist tomorrow; he really seems better and the journey didn't upset him too much. We're so grateful to you all, my dear, thanks seem so inadequate. I hope that we'll see each other again in the not too distant future, and I'll certainly let you know how things go.'

'We'd like to know,' said Celine. 'Mother and Father are out I'm afraid, but I'll tell them you called. Please remember us to—to Mr Seymour and Nicky—I expect he's busy now he's back home.'

'I've not seen him since we got back, but he'll ring later, I expect.'

They said goodbye and Celine hung up. In the kitchen garden, picking peas in the warm sun, she was furious to find herself crying.

She was wandering into the house half an hour later when a Dormobile came chugging up the drive. She put down the basket and went to meet the man getting out of the driving seat. A rather nice man, she decided, young and a bit thin, but with an open face and a great shock of hair.

He said good afternoon in a pleasant hesitant voice and looked over his shoulder, apparently for encouragement, because he went on: 'I daresay you won't want us, but we saw the notice and we thought how nice it would be to sleep in beds just for one night—we usually sleep in this. There are six of us.'

He looked hopefully at her and Celine was reminded of Dusty when he wanted his biscuits. 'All grown-ups?' she asked. 'We've got six rooms . . .'

'Well, actually it's my wife and four kids. They're all small.' He was so anxious that she almost leaned forward to give him a reassuring pat.

'If you want to of course you can stay,' she told him. 'How many rooms would you need?'

'Well, if we could have the baby with us? He's six months old and in a carrycot. And could the other three sleep together?'

She thought rapidly. 'There's a room with twin beds and there's a put-u-up I could take in there. Yes, why not?'

'What do you charge?'

She told him, halving the prices for the children, and asking nothing for the baby. 'And we can give you a meal this evening if you'd like that.'

He hesitated. 'Well, the kids only have a high tea.'

'That's all right—you and your wife can have dinner when they are in bed.' Celine smiled. 'Seventy-five pence for the children's tea—each, of course. Dinner's three pounds fifty, but it's a good one—we've got a very good cook.'

A small fair-headed woman peered out at them. 'It sounds lovely, Jimmy,' she said hopefully. The two of them exchanged smiles and Celine felt a pang of envy.

'Come on in and I'll show you your rooms and then you can put the Dormobile away.'

The children trickled out one by one, small rather shy creatures who took her hands willingly enough as they crossed the hall and went up the stairs.

Celine saw them into their rooms, left them to fetch their things, told the man where to put the Dormobile and went to make tea. Lemonade for the children and some of the little cakes Angela had baked that morning. There wouldn't be much profit out of this lot, she guessed, but to turn them away would have been too unkind.

She took tea into the garden and left them sitting round the shabby wrought iron table, and presently, when they had finished, asked if the children would like to go to the kitchen garden with her while she picked some strawberries. They were shy at first, but presently they began to chatter and run to and fro, peering and poking at everything they saw and making friends with Dusty, who had lumbered out to join them. Celine picked her strawberries, popped one into each small mouth and declared herself ready to go back indoors. 'There's a swing under the mulberry tree,' she suggested, 'if you could get your daddy to start you off.'

She left them reluctantly; it would have been fun to have stayed with them playing in the garden.

She found Angela in the kitchen, explained about the cakes, had a cup of tea and sought advice about the children's high tea. Barney, sitting in his chair by the Aga polishing the silver, advised 'Sandwiches, and a nice boiled egg. There's nothing nicer, Miss Celine.'

'And a jelly for afters,' put in Angela.

'I'd like to give them strawberries, but there aren't enough for everyone.'

'Then I'll 'ave a few for the jelly with a nice topping of cream and some of them little biscuits you made.' Angela poured more tea for Celine. 'And what about dinner?'

'Oh, the usual, I thought. There's plenty of soup, isn't there, or some of those mushrooms done in tiny pancakes—we were going to have those anyway, and then trout—Father caught several, didn't he?—and the strawberries and cream and coffee.'

Celine went away to lay a small table in the dining room. She put a candle on it and later a little posy of flowers because she was a sentimental girl at heart and they looked such a nice couple. She decked the children's table rather more austerely and had it finished just as her mother and father returned.

The family were still in the garden; Celine pointed them out as her mother went into the house. 'And Father, could we spare a half bottle of that white wine you don't like? On the house, I mean?'

'Why not? I hope the children aren't noisy.'

They were as good as gold, eating their way solidly through everything on the table and then going to bed after a bath. And later, when the children and the baby were sleeping, Celine served dinner. She had changed into a pretty sleeveless dress and Barney served the wine in the candlelight and it all looked very romantic. The young people ate everything on their table too, pausing to smile at each other every now and then. It would be lovely to have someone look at you like that, thought Celine, offering coffee, and know that there were four children, all yours, upstairs. Which naturally enough led her to thoughts of Nicky.

It seemed very quiet after the Dormobile had gone. Celine, whisking through the house with the Hoover and clean linen, found herself wishing they had stayed longer. They had had a lovely time, they assured her, and had meant it, and the children had kissed her without being asked. Perhaps she had missed a lot, living in the depths of the country, letting life idle past her—at least, until a couple of weeks ago; and she was quite enjoying her busy life. All the same, being married to Nicky and having a home of her own would be delightful. If only he would telephone, or even write.

He did better than that; he came the next day. Celine had just seen off an elderly clergyman who had arrived quite late on the previous evening and she was clearing the dining room before going upstairs to make ready a room once more. It was a warm day and although it was still early she was far too hot. Going through the hall with a load of dishes, she stopped short at the sight of him. 'Nicky!' she whispered, and the delight was chased from her face as she remembered all the things Oliver had said.

'Nicky,' she said again, and this time with a question in her voice.

He hurried to meet her, took the tray from her and dumped it impatiently on a hall table. 'Darling girl,' he said softly, 'but you knew I'd come.'

'Well, yes—that is, I hoped you would.'

He had been quick to see that look; he held her lightly and kissed her gently. 'You've been doing too much,' he said softly. 'You're pale—was I such a shock?'

'No—no, of course not. I've wanted to talk to you, Nicky . . . Look, will you wait just a minute or two while I see to these things? Better still, go into the sitting-room and I'll get Barney to take in the coffee. There are one or two things I must do . . .'

He frowned. 'I thought you'd be glad to see me?'

'But I am, truly I am, but I must just finish . . .'

He said sulkily: 'O.K. But when can we have some time to ourselves?'

'After lunch—you will stay, won't you?' She went to pick up her tray and said breathlessly: 'Wait there a second.'

She was back in no time at all to usher him into the sitting-room where her parents were occupied, the one with a bowl of flowers, the other with the pile of letters he was reading.

They were surprised, but their manners were perfect; Nicky was made welcome, invited to lunch, asked any number of questions about his father, and they both forbore from wanting to know why he had come. Celine sat there drinking her coffee, in seventh heaven, her face glowing

with happiness, just for the moment oblivious of
Oliver's remarks. She remembered them later while
she was making up the bed, but somehow they
didn't seem important any more. She would tell
Nicky about them, and he would laugh and she
would laugh with him.

She changed her dress for lunch and took
pains with her face and hair. Her mother, glancing
across the table at her, frowned faintly because
she was so obviously a happy girl, and the only
reason for that could be Nicky Seymour, and she
wasn't quite certain of him—a charming young
man, but somewhere at the back of her mind she
was doubtful about him. Even though she
depended so much upon Celine, she still thought
of her as a small girl, needing to be cossetted and
protected.

Lunch over, the Colonel went to his study to
have the nap he always emphatically denied, and
his wife, after a token offer to help clear the table,
wandered off to the small sitting-room, to read
and embroider and doze. Which left Celine and
Nicky.

'Leave those,' he said the moment they were
alone. 'Surely there's someone to do the chores—
why does it always have to be you?' He spoilt it
rather by adding: 'I've come all this way to see
you, the least you can do is spare me an hour or
two.'

She said reasonably: 'But Nicky, I didn't know
you were coming, and I must take these to the
kitchen. Angela and Barney have more than
enough to do between them.'

He shrugged and sauntered through the doors
into the garden. 'Well, I'll be out here when you're

ready—I'll have to leave after tea.'

A tiny voice pointed out that he could have helped her to clear the table: with two it would have been the work of a few minutes; as it was it was quite ten minutes before she joined him.

Being a practical girl she had the basket over her arm, if they went to the kitchen garden she could pick peas while they talked—besides, if she had something to do it would be easier to tell him what Oliver had said.

'What's that thing for?' he wanted to know.

'Peas, for dinner—someone might come later and we have to be ready.'

'I don't believe you think of me at all,' Nicky grumbled. 'Why do you suppose I came? Not to watch you pick peas.' He caught her arm and threw the basket to the ground. 'Darling girl, there's such a lot to plan.' He kissed her expertly. 'Our whole future.'

And that reminded her. She drew back a little and looked up into his face. 'Nicky—Oliver said such a funny thing when he left here. He said you had a wife.'

Nicky's face went slowly red and then paled. After a long moment of silence, Celine said in a wooden voice: 'So it's true . . .' She tried to smile and failed utterly. 'I didn't believe him.'

Nicky pulled himself together with an effort. 'What if I have? We don't get on—we mean to get a divorce.'

She drew away from him. 'But, Nick, we can't . . . you're married!'

He tried to draw her back, but she pulled away. 'Why didn't you tell me?'

'You silly little girl, because it's not important. Good lord, everyone gets divorced these days, no one thinks anything of it.'

'I do.'

'That's because you're buried alive here. Sleeping Beauty waiting to be wakened by the prince.' Nicky smiled, but she found she couldn't smile back at him.

'What had you intended to do?' she asked him in a calm little voice.

His eyes slid away from hers. 'Well, a weekend in Bournemouth for a start, just to see how we got on together, and then a pleasant . . .' ·

'You don't want to marry me?'

'You're a bit naïve, darling,' he said coaxingly. 'Look, let's forget all this—damn Oliver for interfering! Everything would have been fine . . .'

'Not for me, it wouldn't, Nicky.' Celine was managing to keep her voice steady, but she wasn't sure how long she would be able to stay there. All she wanted to do was to run away and hide and scream and cry and thump someone or something really hard. She might feel better then.

'Oh, come on, Celine.' They were standing in the kitchen garden, just inside the door, and she backed away once more, but Nicky took her arm and pulled her towards him. 'You're being a silly prudish girl.' His voice held impatience. 'Just let me show you . . .'

'Very unwise,' said Oliver gently, and came through the door as he spoke.

'It's my opinion that it might be better for all of us—and that means you as well—if you don't try to show anyone anything. I think the best thing is for you to get into your car and go. Now!'

He placed a gentle compelling hand on Celine's arm and pushed her just as gently through the door. 'Go and have a good cry somewhere,' he advised her. 'We'll have a little chat later.'

She started to walk away and heard Nicky's furious voice and Oliver's quiet calm one. It was just like being in a nightmare and for the moment she hadn't a thought in her head, only a numbness. She walked down the drive, past the Aston Martin and out of the gate, then she turned uphill, away from the village. Oliver was quite right, she was going to have a good cry, but preferably in solitude. Halfway up the hill she climbed a gate and went into a copse. It was cool and dim here and there was no sound except for the wood-pigeons and the rooks. She took the narrow path between the trees and the field beyond and sat down on a hummock of grass. She could see the house and its gardens very clearly below her, and presently she watched a figure who could only be Nicky get into his car and drive away. She started to cry then, and she went on crying until there were no tears left and her hanky so sodden that she had to use the hem of her skirt. She didn't feel much better, only empty and sad and hopeless. Nothing mattered any more, and when she heard footsteps presently she didn't turn round. She knew who it was: Oliver was a man who was hard to get away from, or so it seemed. She wondered briefly how it was that he was here at all.

'Why did you come?' she asked without turning her head. 'And how did you know that I was here?' Her voice was still thick from all her crying.

'He told his wife he had to come here to collect something he'd left behind.' He sat down beside her. 'And I could see you up here from the house.'

She stared out over the fields. 'Did Nicky . . . did he say anything?'

'Nothing. You won't see him again, Celine.'

'But he must have said something . . . I mean,' she hesitated, trying to find the right words, 'if he's going to divorce his wife he—he might want to see me again—he said he . . .' She stopped, because she had been going to say that Nicky had told her he loved her, but he very surely never had.

'He's not going to divorce her—she intends to divorce him before she becomes a nervous wreck. And he doesn't love you, Celine, just as he's never loved any of the other girls in his life.'

Oliver had flung an arm round her shoulders and she found it comforting.

'I suppose it's because you aren't interested in women that you're easy to talk to—like an uncle.'

He took this unflinchingly on the chin. 'Very likely, in which case perhaps I might be allowed to give some avuncular advice. You have to shut the door on these last few weeks and never open it again. You must forget, and the easiest way is to go from here and get a job where you work so hard all day that you sleep, exhausted, all night.'

Celine blew her beautiful nose with resounding resolution. 'That's all very well, but it's impossible to leave Mother and Father to cope—after all, I started it all . . .'

He sounded quite unworried. 'Is there anyone who could take your place for a few weeks? A cousin or an aunt or an old school friend?'

She said reluctantly: 'There's an aunt—my mother's much younger sister. She lives in Bridport—she's a widow.'

'Would your mother and father object if this could be arranged?'

'No, I don't know—I suppose not—as long as they didn't get too involved. And anyway, I don't want them to know . . .'

He was soothing. 'Of course not. All the same, if you'll let me talk to them it would make it easier. I could see this aunt too . . .'

'If you want to.' Her voice was small. 'I don't really care—I'd like to die!'

'Self-pity will get you nowhere. And don't look at me like that—consider me as a necessary evil and make the best of it.' He passed her a very large white handkerchief and she blew her nose and mopped her face once more. 'I know of a job.'

'Where?' she asked listlessly.

'Bethnal Green. I'm a paediatrician—I do most of my work in hospitals, but I've started this follow-up clinic because I find that over the years, a number of patients never return for check-ups, mostly because the hospital is too far away, the fares are too much, the baby can't be left or there's no one to mind the children. The clinic has helped solve this problem, it's easy to get at for anyone living in the East End and the waiting time isn't too long. I've got two nurses and a couple of partners there, but we need help—another pair of hands to dress and undress the children, take their particulars, find notes and run errands. I'm not there all the time, of course, but it would be a whole day's work for you.' He added thoughtfully:

'But perhaps it wouldn't do—you've led a sheltered life here, haven't you?'

Celine was feeling wretchedly miserable, but that stung her. 'You're only saying that because you think I'm . . . I thought he loved me and we'd be married. I suppose if I'd had a job and met a lot of people I'd have known. Well, I won't make the same mistake twice, the next time I'll have it in writing.' She sounded quite fierce, but her rage subsided as quickly as it had come. She said with pathetic dignity, 'I'm quite capable of hard work and I don't care in the least what I do. If things can be fixed here, I'll take the job.'

'Good.' Oliver sounded neither surprised nor pleased. 'The hours are long and irregular, and you'll be paid fifty pounds a week. There's a room over the surgery where you can live rent free, and you'll get a luncheon voucher.' He got to his feet and pulled her to hers. 'We'll go back now and I'll have a talk with your mother and father while you wash your face. Do you think you'll want to weep any more, or will you be able to discuss your future sensibly?'

She seethed. 'You really are horrible!' she began, but he wasn't listening.

'You're a big girl, aren't you? That'll help a lot at the surgery. Oh, don't worry, no one will harm you, but they won't bully you either; in any case, I shouldn't allow that.'

They were retracing their steps and Celine studied the massive back going ahead of her. He was a very large man, but not only that, he was very sure of himself, she simply couldn't imagine anyone trying to get the better of him.

They reached the house, not hurrying, and she

went to her room, leaving him to find his own way. As they parted in the hall she said ungraciously: 'I suppose you want to stay the night?'

He studied her face, pale and pink-eyed. 'Suppose we leave that for the moment?' he suggested mildly.

She went on upstairs. In truth, she didn't care what he did. He seemed to have taken over her immediate future without any trouble, and she was too unhappy to do anything about it. After all, she could always come home, and perhaps Aunt Chloe from Bridport wouldn't want to work her fingers to the bone, even for a few weeks. It would be a pity to go, she mused, splashing cold water on to her puffy face, the bed and breakfast business had got off to a good start and there was no reason to suppose it would peter out. Barney and Angela knew the ropes now and her mother and father had accepted it. But Oliver, overbearing and always right, had hit on the solution. Celine blinked back fresh tears, made up her face and did her hair, then went downstairs. She wanted to turn and run when she reached the hall, but Oliver must have heard her step on the stairs; he came to meet her and shepherded her into her father's study, his hand firm and reassuring on her shoulder.

CHAPTER FOUR

CELINE had no idea what Oliver had told her parents—indeed, she didn't much care, but whatever it was, he had smoothed the way for her. Beyond her mother's 'Darling!' and her father's 'Sorry this had to happen, my dear', they said nothing, only plunged at once into the plans Oliver had suggested.

'There's no reason at all why Chloe shouldn't come for a time,' declared her Mother. 'She loves organising and Angela and Barney like her. I'll telephone and see what she says, though she'll want a day or two to get organised, you know.'

'That should do very well, Mrs Baylis—I'll come down in a week's time and fetch Celine,' and when Celine made a small denying movement: 'The surgery isn't easy to find unless you're familiar with the East End—it will save a lot of trouble if I take you straight there. There's a caretaker living over the clinic and she can take Celine round the place.' He turned to look at Celine, sitting silently with a rigid face. 'That is, if you still feel you're up to it?'

'Of course I am. A change will be very—very pleasant.'

'I hope you'll find it so.' He got to his feet. 'And now I must be going. Shall I give you a ring tomorrow morning and see how things are?'

'You're not staying for the night?' asked Celine,

and had the curious feeling that her lifeline had been cut.

'Afraid not,' he smiled at her kindly.

'Not even for dinner?'

'Er—no. I'm sorry.' He shook hands with Mrs Baylis and the Colonel, but he only smiled again at Celine and waved a casual hand, so that she didn't go to the door with them, but stayed sitting in her chair. It was a pity she seemed quite unable to think properly; she still felt empty and numb, and the wish to have another weep was very strong.

But not possible. Her mother and father were barely back in the room before a car turned into the drive. 'Customers,' said her mother with satisfaction and a barely concealed relief because she didn't know what to say to Celine. The whole miserable matter would have to be mentioned sooner or later, and later was preferable.

The couple who got out of the car looked around them with critical eyes before they addressed Celine, waiting in the porch.

'Got room for three of us?' asked the man without bothering to say good afternoon. 'Me and the missus and the kid? He can sleep with us.'

'I'm afraid we haven't any rooms with three beds,' said Celine, wishing they would go away.

'What's the damage, then?'

She told him, and because she didn't care if they stayed or not, charged the full price for the child. Rather to her surprise he didn't object but nodded briskly. 'O.K. Anyone to take the bags?'

'Yes. I'll show you the rooms if you'd like to come inside.'

She didn't like the wife very much either—far too fat in jeans and a striped shirt and a great deal

of jewellery, and she didn't like the child at all
when he got out of the back of the car, a boy of
ten years or so with a discontented face and a
whiny voice. She took them to the east wing,
listened politely to their comments about the out-
of-date plumbing and the funny old furniture,
agreed to give them dinner and went to tell Barney
to get their bags. She had a feeling they were going
to be tiresome, and she was right; the boy whined
for fish and chips, his father loudly voiced his
disappointment at not being able to have his pint
before dinner, and his wife pushed the peas Angela
had picked from the garden on to the side of her plate
and declared that there was nothing to beat frozen
veg; she couldn't abide stuff straight from a garden.

Celine, not really caring what they had to say,
put the newly picked strawberries back in the
fridge and took in dishes of ice cream—the only
item on the menu they all appeared to enjoy.
Feeling mean about the strawberries, she offered
second helpings of ice cream and met their
approving looks with remorse.

The boy stayed up after dinner, roaming the
house, teasing Dusty and making a nuisance of
himself, and when Celine pointed out in her
politest manner that they might have the sitting
room for their use until they went to bed, they did
nothing to restrain the boy. She saw them go next
morning with real relief; she had spent an almost
sleepless night and their unreasonable demands for
this and that in the morning had quite worn her
out.

She had had time enough to think during the
night, for, tired though she was, she was unable to
sleep. She lay thinking of Nicky, wondering what

he was doing and where he was and whether he
had ever loved her at all. Oliver had said he
hadn't, and although she didn't want to believe
him she was aware that he wasn't a man to lie. All
the same, it was a bitter pill to swallow. She filled
the day with a good deal of quite unnecessary
work, spent several hours in the garden and went
in for tea to face, at last, her parents' gentle
questions. They were upset for her sake, but she
sensed that they neither of them had liked Nicky
very much and her mother at least was relieved
that the whole sorry affair was over.

Mrs Baylis had had a long telephone conversation with her sister and presently embarked
thankfully on to the plans they had for the next
few weeks. Everything would be splendid, declared
Mrs Baylis. Chloe would come for as long as she
was needed, so Celine mustn't feel she had to rush
back home. It seemed that Oliver had telephoned
Aunt Chloe too, and that lady, impressed by his
quiet assured voice stating such sensible reasons
for Celine to leave home for a while, had entered
into the plans with enthusiasm and would be with
them in five days' time, so that Celine could give
her some idea how to run the bed and breakfast
business.

To all of which Celine listened quietly, agreed
with her father that the job at Bethnal Green
sounded interesting, assured him that she would
have quite enough money to live comfortably, and
took herself off to the garden again, to be
interrupted within the hour by a charming elderly
couple who were delighted with the house, their
room, and the dinner she presently served them.
The Colonel, wandering through the hall, had met

them and been so taken with the old gentleman that he had produced a good claret to go with their meal and after dinner had strolled with him through the gardens, while Mrs Baylis and his wife chatted pleasantly in the drawing room.

'If only they were all like that,' sighed Mrs Baylis, watching their beautifully kept elderly car going down the drive. She took Celine's arm. 'Darling, are we making money?'

'Yes—not a great deal, but enough to feed us all, pay the wages and put some by. Father's kept the accounts, you know, and he's banked quite a nice sum—it's worth it, Mother. I feel mean leaving you, though, just as we're getting started.'

'Nonsense, darling. You've got it all running so smoothly and your aunt is a splendid manager and good with people—well, you have to be, don't you? I expect you'll meet any number of types at the surgery.'

Celine said quietly: 'Yes, I expect so.' She didn't really care.

'And you'll come back feeling quite yourself, darling.'

She forced herself to say, 'Yes, Mother,' in a cheerful voice, because that was what her mother wanted to hear.

The days went by. There was a good deal to do—lists to make for Aunt Chloe, menus to make out for Angela, shopping to be done, and if she didn't sleep soundly at night no one knew. Celine grew a little thin and there were shadows under her lovely eyes, but when Aunt Chloe arrived, she met her cheerfully enough and spent a whole day with her, making sure she knew what she was letting herself in for. They had had a few quiet days, but now, on the same day as Aunt Chloe, a party of six arrived, making excellent material for her to practise on, as well as convincing her that she hadn't left her comfortable house in Bridport for nothing.

And two days later, Oliver arrived. Celine had just ushered three young women to their rooms, and when she got downstairs again, there he was, standing in the hall, talking to her mother and father.

His hullo was noncommittal, friendly and rather casual. 'Ready to leave in the morning?' he wanted to know. 'Can you put me up for the night? I see you're busy.'

'Yes, of course there's a room. There are only those three ladies, and it's getting a bit late for anyone else.'

'You'll be our guest,' said her father. 'We dine a little later than any guests who may be here. Come into the study and tell me how your uncle is faring—I've got some good malt whisky . . .'

And that was almost all Celine saw of Oliver that evening, for conversation was general at the dinner table, and as soon as the meal was over she excused herself. Breakfast had to be laid and she had to check that everything was as it should be in the kitchen. Angela and Barney were coping well, but Mrs Stokes's help wasn't quite enough; next week they must see about getting more help from the village. She had already talked to her mother about it, and reminded Aunt Chloe to bear it in mind.

That lady had taken to the chores like a duck to water, and Celine had noticed that she was on the best of terms with Oliver—indeed, she hadn't offered to help in the dining-room but had stayed talking with the others, and as Celine went out of the dining-room she felt pettishly that she had done more than her share of the work that evening. After all, Oliver had come to fetch her, and there was still a lot she wanted to know. She went slowly into the hall and wandered to the front door, still standing open. Well, if he chose to ignore her, he could for all she cared. She had taken barely a dozen steps when he came unhurriedly out of the door.

'The best time of the day for a stroll in the garden,' he observed cheerfully, and took her arm.

She stood still. 'It's very pleasant, but I'm just on my way to bed—I'm tired . . .' Her voice had risen as well as being sharp.

'And sorry for yourself. Poor little you, doing all the work while we sit around gossiping.'

'I'm not little!' she snapped, and tried to take her arm away—something quite impossible, and it would have been undignified to tug at it.

'No, you're not. You're quite a big girl, aren't you? I believe I said that before. You'll be a lot more tired after a day's work at the surgery. I suspect you'll dislike me there even more than you do now.'

'How do you know that I . . . I don't dislike you, not any more, you've—you've been very kind and I'm grateful.'

'Save your gratitude until you've been in Bethnal Green for a couple of weeks.' He was walking her between the rose-beds towards the sundial at the back of the house. 'You look so right here among the flowers—I wonder if I'm doing right, taking you away from all this?'

'Oh, yes, you are!' Celine sounded almost frantic. 'You wouldn't change your mind now? I'll work hard, I will really . . . I must get away!'

'I know that.' Oliver stopped and looked down into her face. 'It's still a deep hurt, isn't it? You poor girl—and I won't make it worse by telling you you'll get over it.'

He sounded kind. Celine, struggling against a desire to burst into tears, sniffed, and he passed her a handkerchief without comment.

'A lovely evening,' he observed, taking no notice of the sniffs. 'This is a delightful spot, and you'll miss it, of course, but the stars are the same.' He stopped again and tilted his head. 'Look, you can pick any one you like and call it yours and know it's just as clearly seen here as it is in Bethnal Green. Have that bright one straight above your head.' And when she looked up obediently: 'It's your midsummer star, and it will always be there, like a fairy godmother.'

'Don't be ridiculous—you surely don't believe in fairies?'

'Perhaps not fairies, but certainly in kindly fate. One day you'll believe that too, Celine—but not yet. Now, off to bed with you, we're leaving after breakfast.'

He walked her briskly back to the house, and once inside wished her goodnight equally briskly, but his eyes lingered on her tired unhappy face and he added: 'I'll say goodnight to everyone for you, shall I?' And when she nodded, he turned away and went into the drawing-room.

They left at mid-morning and Oliver tactfully wandered off while Celine said goodbye to her mother and father, then he got into the car and drove her away before there was time to have second thoughts, entertaining her with a mild flow of conversation which gave her little time to herself. As they threaded their way through the beginnings of Bagshot he slowed. 'I think we'll stop for lunch,' he observed. 'I don't know about you, but I'm hungry.'

Celine had no appetite at all, but she was too polite to say so. He took her to Pennyhill Park, and once in the Latymer Room she was forced to admit to herself that the food on the menu looked tempting, and with almost no breakfast inside her, lunch was a must, and once started on delicious lobster patties, tournedos Rossini, and a delicious ice cream, she discovered that she was hungry after all.

Once they reached London she was a little daunted to find that Oliver intended driving straight through the heart of the city; even though the rush hour was still a couple of hours away, there was plenty of traffic, but he didn't seem to mind. He drove on steadily until they reached the Mile End Road and turned away from the river towards Victoria Park, but only for a few minutes. Presently he turned off the busy road and wound his way through a jungle of narrow back streets, lined with small shabby houses, overshadowed by tower blocks. Celine sat without speaking; somehow she hadn't imagined it quite like this. She thought of home and the endless garden and the fields beyond and felt lost. She didn't see Oliver's sideways glance at her tense face.

'Rather different, isn't it?' he observed easily. 'We're lucky, you and I, to have somewhere pleasant to live.'

For the sake of something to say, she asked: 'Oh, do you live in the country too?'

He hesitated for a second. 'I've a house at Chiswick, by the river, it's surprisingly quiet there.'

He was driving slowly, edging past parked cars, children playing in the street, gossiping groups spilling off the pavements. He reached a corner, turned it and stopped before a bleak building which none the less had clean windows and fresh paintwork.

'Here we are.' He leaned across and opened her door for her and got out himself. Celine stood on the pavement for a moment, looking around her. It was a busy street, full of tatty shops, some of them empty, and small brick houses, all exactly alike. The pavements were crowded and quite a few people had stopped to stare; most of them appeared to know Oliver, for there was a chorus of, 'Ullo, Doc', as he crossed the pavement and opened the door. There was a big painted board nailed to the wall, proclaiming the surgery hours and the telephone number, and Celine stopped to read it before she followed him inside.

The passage was narrow, painted cream with a cheerful red-tiled floor, and there was a pot plant on a wall bracket, spilling vivid geraniums. The doors were primrose yellow and there seemed to be any number of them. Oliver passed them all and opened the door facing them at the end of the passage. The room was at the back of the house, with a window overlooking a very small back yard, paved and dotted with concrete bowls filled with more geraniums. The room was bright with cream paint and distempered walls. It had two desks in it, at one of which sat a woman in nurse's uniform. She had sharp features, wiry grey hair and an air of great energy.

She looked up as Oliver opened the door and ushered Celine in, and smiled widely. 'Right on time!' she exclaimed approvingly. 'I'll get tea at once, Dr Seymour.'

'Meet Celine Baylis,' said Oliver. 'Celine, this is my right hand and prop, Sister Griffiths—my left hand, Nurse Byng, is on holiday. We shall all be glad of a willing slave, won't we, Maggie?'

'Indeed we shall. Are you taking the clinic this evening, Doctor?'

Oliver had gone to the desk and was bending over the stack of post. 'Yes, why not? David could do with some help, I expect.' He glanced up at Celine, standing uncertainly at the door still. 'Sit down, Celine—when we've had a cup of tea I'll get Mrs Thatch to take you to your room and show you round.'

There wasn't much time wasted over tea, and the conversation was confined to Celine and Sister Griffiths because Oliver was reading his letters and frowning over forms. Celine found herself dismissed with kindly detachment, to be led away by Mrs Thatch, a cheerful Cockney body who had the top floor flat, where she lived with her husband. 'There's a nice room for you, ducks,' she told Celine, leading the way up the narrow staircase. 'A bed-sit all ter yerself. I'll bring yer breakfast and yer supper and tidy up like. There's a gas ring if yer want a cuppa, and a washbasin. Classy, I call it.'

Never mind what Mrs Thatch called it, thought Celine, looking round the room she was ushered into; it was a far cry from her room at home. It had all the comforts, it was true, and indeed there was a washbasin and a gas ring and a partitioned-off corner with kettle, saucepan and crockery neatly stowed; the curtains were pretty too, matching the spread which disguised the divan bed, but looking at it, she was suddenly homesick for her own elegant bedroom. 'It's very nice,' she told her companion, and managed a smile. 'Is there a bathroom?'

'Lor' bless yer, yes,' declared her companion. ' 'Ot and cold too, all day and all night. There's two more rooms on the landing—no one in 'em though—nurse Byng goes 'ome each evening and Sister Griffiths has got a flat, but you've no need to be nervous—me and Alf, we're always upstairs.' She looked at Celine's Gucci case on the bed. 'I'll leave yer ter unpack, miss. I daresay the doctor'll 'ave some work for yer later.'

Left to herself, Celine hung her clothes in the built-in cupboard along one wall, arranged everything else in the drawers in the dressing table, tidied her person, did her face and hair, then went downstairs and through the door at the bottom opening into the hall. And all this while she hadn't allowed herself to think about Nicky. All the doors were shut; she went to the room she had been in and knocked.

Oliver's 'Come in' sounded impatient, and: 'Don't knock,' he told her, barely raising his head from the desk. He nodded towards a door behind him. 'That's my office; just walk in and out if you want something.' He raised his voice. 'Maggie, take Celine round the place, will you? There's time before we open.'

He didn't look up as Sister Griffiths appeared and led Celine away.

The building was surprisingly big—an old house, gutted inside and rebuilt according to Oliver's plans, Sister Griffiths explained, opening and shutting doors on to waiting room, examination rooms, sterilising room, a small well-equipped first aid room, a spotless kitchenette, even a bathroom. At Celine's look of surprise Sister Griffiths said dryly: 'It's often quicker to bath a small child—if they're grubby Dr Seymour can't always examine easily.'

She glanced at Celine, who had said nothing at all during their tour of inspection. 'Do you think you'll like it? It's hard work—you'll have all kinds of dirty jobs to do, you know—general dogsbody, as it were. And the hours are irregular.'

'Yes, I—I was told that. I'd like to try it though and I'll do my best.'

Sister Griffiths nodded. 'I'm sure you will—nothing else would suit Dr Seymour. You look a big strong girl, thank heaven. Well, if you've seen everything, we'd better go back—we open shortly. I think it might be best if you stay with me this evening so you get some idea of what goes on.'

The waiting room was already half full: Sister Griffiths, with the assured ease of long practice, sorted patients, took names, found notes and dropped a swift: 'Get their coats off, will you, Celine? And hats if they're wearing them. Several of them will need to be undressed—you can do that while Dr Seymour's talking to the mothers.'

So Celine found herself dressing and undressing small unwilling children while Oliver, looking quite different and somehow very remote, sat at his desk, talking to the mothers, and presently, because she was tired and unhappy, the evening became a blur of trying to be quick and remembering many names and carrying out Oliver's simple instructions.

The surgery seemed to go on for hours, and when it finally ended, there was the clearing up to do, chairs to be put straight, towels to be replaced, the floor to clean—tasks which fell to Celine's lot, since Sister Griffiths was fully occupied with the first aid room and the surgery itself. There was no sign of Oliver, but presently she heard his voice, calling Sister Griffiths, and a few minutes later that lady appeared again.

'Well, I'm for home,' she said cheerfully. 'Not so bad, was it? A nice easy evening, actually. We start at half past eight tomorrow, so you must be here by eight o'clock.' She walked to the door, looking not in the least tired. 'You did very well,' she added kindly. 'See you tomorrow.'

Celine said goodnight with a cheerfulness she didn't feel, finished emptying the wastepaper baskets into the bin outside the back door and took off the blue overall she had been wearing. She felt hot and grubby and cross; surely they could have left her to settle in on her first evening instead of taking it for granted that she would plunge head first into a job she knew nothing about? She hung up the overall behind the door and started for the stairs. It was half past eight and she hoped devoutly that there was supper somewhere beyond them.

She had opened the door and had her foot on the bottom step when suddenly Oliver's office door opened. 'Finished?' he asked. 'We're early this evening. Go and do your face and I'll take you out to dinner.'

'How kind,' said Celine, rather coldly, 'but there'll be supper waiting for me, and I'm tired.'

'So am I—all the more reason to eat,' he smiled at her kindly. 'You did very well, so Maggie tells me. Now run and wash or whatever—five minutes enough?'

For some reason quite beyond her comprehension, she agreed meekly that five minutes was quite enough.

She didn't bother much with make-up, but brushed her hair smooth, dabbed powder on her nose and went down to meet him; if he didn't like her like that he had himself to blame, she hadn't wanted to go, anyway.

It was disconcerting to her that he barely glanced in her direction, but opened the door, locked it carefully behind him, and saw her into the car. 'We're not going far,' he told her. 'There's a pub not too far away where we can get a good meal.'

The pub was a Victorian red brick monstrosity in the middle of a long busy street. Oliver manoeuvred the car between a van and a dilapidated banger, got out and opened her door. That he had been there before was obvious, for he went unhesitatingly through the door marked Saloon Bar, nodded a greeting to the shirt-sleeved bartender and went ahead of her to a small table in a corner where he pulled out a chair for her and then sat down opposite.

'I come here from time to time,' he explained casually. 'What would you like to drink?'

The food was good—roast beef, Yorkshire pudding, roast potatoes and cabbage and a trifle afterwards. Not a meal Celine would have chosen on a warm summer's evening, but once it was set before her, she discovered that she was hungry, and ate with an appetite to match her companion's.

And while they ate, he talked about the clinic, elaborating on the rather sparse instructions she had had that evening, explaining when she could expect to be free and which day she could have each week. 'There's just one thing,' he told her, 'I'd prefer you not to go out alone in the evenings—get someone to go with you and see you back.'

'But I don't know anyone!' She went faintly pink. 'Well, I've a few friends in London, but I don't expect they'd know how to get here.'

He smiled at her. 'Well, we'll worry about that later. I don't see why you shouldn't have a weekend free occasionally so that you can go home.'

'Oh, that would be super!'

'But not just yet. We don't want to lose sight of the reason for your coming here, do we?'

Celine picked up her coffee cup with a hand which shook slightly. 'No.'

Oliver's voice was very even. 'You don't believe me now, but after a week or two of working here, you'll be tired enough not to dream about Nicky, and later, when you've got into your stride, he won't matter any more.'

She stared at him, her eyes bright with tears she wasn't going to shed. 'What do you know about it?' she asked bitterly. 'You go around arranging other people's lives for them; I daresay you're well-meaning, but you've no right . . .'

He said placidly: 'You're tired. I'll take you back.' There was nothing in his manner to show if he was annoyed with her; he chatted amiably as they returned and his goodnight as he unlocked the door and ushered her inside was perfectly friendly. Celine did find herself fretting about it as she got ready for bed; she didn't really know him at all—indeed, he occupied her thoughts so thoroughly that she forgot all about Nicky.

But not for long. Slogging her way through a day of unaccustomed tasks, she found herself daydreaming; Nicky miraculously not married after all, arriving on the doorstep and taking her away; Nicky ringing up, even writing a letter. He didn't know where she was, of course—common sense reared a prosaic head for a few seconds, but had no chance. At the back of her mind she was aware that she was behaving like a silly schoolgirl, and perhaps if she had been at home and could have gone for a walk with Dusty all the nonsense would have been blown out of her head. As it was, her dreams took a firm hold as she tidied up, emptied bowls, consoled weeping infants, took small clothes off and put them on again and generally made herself as useful as she knew how. Oliver wasn't there. David Slater, his partner, a stocky young man with a nice face, introduced himself when he arrived a few minutes before the clinic was due to open.

Celine was on the point of asking where Oliver was and stopped just in time—it was no business of hers and she really didn't care. She had said she would take the job for a few weeks because it would help her to get over the smart of Nicky's behaviour, and she would stay, but that didn't prevent the daydreams. The moment she was free she would go and see him; Oliver couldn't prevent her doing that, and she had Mrs Seymour's address.

She was free for a couple of hours after lunch, a snack meal shared with Sister Griffiths in the office. 'Why not go out for an hour?' asked that lady. 'The bus I take goes past Victoria Park, and you can take one back here almost to the door.'

It seemed a good idea. Celine spent an hour or more exploring the park and discovered it to be a pleasant place, and when she got back it was to find Mrs Thatch arranging a tray of tea things in the office. 'Sister Griffiths doesn't 'ave 'er tea 'ere,' she explained, 'being able to 'ave it in 'er own 'ome. I've done yer a nice bit o' toast.' She retired to the door. 'And eat it all, miss, evening is busy.'

Celine ate it all while she went over the jobs she might be expected to do that evening; speed, common sense and patience seemed to be the essentials, and a knowledge of where to find everything. Presently she carried the tray back upstairs, tidied herself in her room and went back to the waiting room. There was half an hour before the clinic opened and the room was far too warm, even empty. She opened a window or two, put on her overall and settled down to leaf through some of the magazines laid out on the centre table.

The telephone interrupted this; Oliver's placid voice telling her that he would be late and would she tell Sister Griffiths to get on with what she could. He didn't say more than that, but rang off, leaving her feeling she was a very small cog in the wheels of his working day.

He was more than half an hour late, but he
showed no signs of hurry as he came in. He went
straight to the waiting room, looked round at the
harassed mothers and their impatient children,
apologised with a smile that took the peevish look
off several faces, and went to the surgery.

The clinic was full. Celine, performing her
mundane tasks, began to think they would never
reach the last patient. She had blown noses,
mopped up tears and worse, found lost garments
and run to and fro fetching and carrying for Sister
Griffiths and occasionally for Oliver. Now she was
tired; too tired to think of anything other than
supper and bed.

Climbing thankfully between the sheets several
hours later, she reflected that that was exactly
what Oliver had told her. She frowned; the
wretched man was always right—she was asleep
before she could think what to do about it.

It was surprising what a long dreamless sleep
did for one. Celine peered out of her window upon
a glorious morning, put on a thin sleeveless dress,
did her face and hair with extra care and ate the
splendid breakfast Mrs Thatch had provided. The
surroundings might be pretty grim, but the clinic
building and its appointments were beyond
complaint, as was the food. I shall get fat, thought
Celine as she began on the early morning chores.
She was halfway through the day's work before
she remembered it would be Saturday tomorrow—
emergencies only in the morning and then free
until Monday morning. She wasn't going home, it
was too short a time anyway. She would wait for
the weekend Oliver had promised her, and besides,
they were doing splendidly with the bed and

breakfasts—house full, her mother had declared over the phone, and Aunt Chloe was loving every minute of it. And to her mother's enquiries as to how she was enjoying her job, Celine had replied that she was loving it. Strangely enough, upon reflection, she found this was almost true, probably because she had no time to think about anything except things like where someone's notes were, and what Sister Griffiths had done with her scissors and where were the particular forms Oliver was asking for.

She saw very little of him. True, he paused on his way in or out and asked how she was getting on, reminded her about not going out alone at night and mentioned, vaguely, the weekend he had promised, but beyond that she was a faceless pair of hands, fetching and carrying.

The morning clinic on Saturday passed without incident and Sister Griffiths departed for home just after noon, leaving Celine to have her dinner at the little table in her room and then go to the park again. She stayed there for tea and went back on the bus to find her supper waiting for her. 'And me and Thatch is going out this evening, so if yer want ter watch telly, you're welcome. Leave them dishes in the sink if you will, miss.'

It was a dull evening, Celine wrote letters, watched a show on T.V., without seeing it, and went early to bed with a book. The house was very quiet without the Thatch's cheerful voices; she was quite glad to hear them come in just before midnight. Tomorrow, she thought, sitting up in bed with the book still unopened, she would go out for the whole day. She had money; her pay packet had been handed to her that morning by

Sister Griffiths. She would go to church—St Paul's, perhaps—and then lunch at a small restaurant and spend the afternoon in Green Park. She could have tea there and then have a meal at another restaurant before taking a bus back.

The Thatches didn't get up very early on Sundays. Celine was dressed and ready by the time her breakfast arrived. She had taken extra pains with her make-up and put on silk separates, not new but of an expensive simplicity. Mrs Thatch eyed her with open admiration. 'My, you do look a treat, miss,' she declared. 'You'll 'ave the men running after you, an' no mistake.' She added darkly: 'An' just you take care!'

There were very few people on the streets. Celine got on her bus, went to St Paul's and afterwards took a bus to Green Park, to find to her dismay that most of the restaurants in the area were closed. In the end she settled for a meal at a Golden Egg and presently crossed Piccadilly into Green Park. It was a heavenly day. She found a seat and read the paper she had bought, and presently strolled off to find a tea-room. Several men had stopped to speak to her; she had replied to them all with chilly politeness and gone on her way, not in the least disconcerted. She was aware that she was nice to look at and she supposed that if she were a man she might be tempted to chat up a passable girl.

She had tea and started back towards Piccadilly. There was, she remembered from previous shopping expeditions with her mother, a decent small restaurant somewhere near Old Bond Street. There was the chance that it would be open for dinner, if not she would have to make do with another

Golden Egg. As she walked she began to go through the names of various friends who lived in London. It might be a good idea to give some of them a ring and perhaps meet them on an occasional Sunday. She was, she confessed to herself, most dreadfully lonely.

She had come out of the Park and was about to cross Piccadilly when she looked up and saw Nicky coming towards her.

CHAPTER FIVE

CELINE closed her eyes and then opened them again. Nicky was still there. A moment later she felt his hand on her shoulders, and heard him say: 'Darling girl—of all the miracles! Is it actually you? I've dreamed of you so often I'm afraid I shall wake up . . .'

She smiled shakily. 'Yes, it's me. You're—you're the last person I expected to see, Nicky.' She took a steadying breath. 'In fact, I came to London to forget about you.'

He laughed. 'But fate didn't intend that, did she?' He took her arm. 'Where are you going? On second thoughts I don't want to know. You're going to have dinner with me and we'll talk—there's so much to say.'

'No, there's not, Nicky. You're married . . .'

He interrupted her quickly. 'I've left her for good—I'll get a divorce and we'll get married, and until then we can see each other every day.' He had crossed Piccadilly, taking her with him.

'Anyway, we can't talk here, I know just the place.'

Celine's head told her she was being more than foolish, her heart egged her on to go with him. After all, there was no harm in listening to what he had to say, and had she not longed to see him?

The restaurant was tucked away in a side street, small, discreet and dimly lighted, and even if Celine hadn't been romantic it would have made her so, and when she made a protest, a not very strong one, Nicky took her hand and said gently: 'No, don't argue, darling. We'll have a drink and you shall tell me what you're doing in London, and after that——' he gave her hand a squeeze, 'we'll talk about our future.'

It was hard to resist him. She let him order for both of them, drank the wine poured into her glass and allowed herself to be happy. It was a pity that underneath the happiness, buried deep but still there, was doubt.

Nicky saw the doubt. He talked amusingly about everything under the sun excepting themselves, dismissed her queries about his father with a shrug and a smile and a casual: 'Well, you know how it is with the elderly—he's doing quite well.' He gave her his disarming smile again. 'But I want to know about you, Celine.'

'I'm working for Oliver,' she said, 'at his surgery in Bethnal Green,' and saw with a pang of uneasiness that his face had become ugly with some strong emotion. 'I like it,' she added. 'It's hard work but very interesting.'

'I might have known! All my life I've had to put up with Oliver interfering with me. I suppose he's been jealous.' He glanced at Celine and went on carefully: 'He's never been much of a success socially—too cocksure, I suppose. The times he's come between me and my friends—even my wife. Ah well, one should be sorry for him, I suppose, poor devil.'

'Why is he a poor devil?' Celine asked; she had never thought of Oliver in that light, certainly not as a man to be pitied. And he had been kind to her. It struck her that she rather liked him after all. She said quite sharply, 'I don't think he needs pity, he's dependable and kind and . . .'

Nicky's eyes narrowed. 'Darling, don't get ideas about him—you belong to me, you know.'

'No, I don't. Nicky, I'd like to go now. Thank you for my dinner, it was very nice. I'll catch a bus . . .'

She had expected him to ignore that and get a taxi and perhaps drive back with her, but he said sulkily: 'Oh, very well—there's a bus stop across the road, but don't think you can shake me off like this, darling—you gave me enough encouragement to start with, you know. I shall come looking for you.'

'No, don't do that. I'd rather not see you again. It—it's all quite pointless, and I want to stop now, so let's say goodbye, Nicky.'

He didn't answer her but took her arm, crossed the road and got to the bus stop just as one came into sight. It wasn't the one she wanted, but now she wanted to get away as quickly as possible. He barely waited for her to get on, and when she called goodbye, she heard, his 'Au revoir,' with mixed feelings.

Back in her room, she sat down to think. She should have been happy and elated; she had been longing to see Nicky again and now that she had she wasn't happy at all. Undoubtedly he had been glad to see her, but his snide remarks about Oliver had worried her, and his lack of interest in his father—that was another thing which bothered her. He was as charming as ever, she admitted that, but when she was away from him the charm didn't work as well as it should have done. Perhaps that was because she had no time to think about him any more. At home it had been easy enough to sit and dream. She tried to decide what she would do if he came to her and told her that he had got his divorce and wanted to marry her, but she couldn't. His wife, a shadowy figure in her daydreams, had become flesh and blood a woman with feelings like her own. Celine sighed and went to bed. She would have to be up early and even if she didn't sleep she would have to rest.

And she didn't sleep; an hour here and an hour there, not enough to blot out the dark shadows under her eyes and put colour in her cheeks. And she was so muddle-headed in her work that morning that Sister Griffiths was sharp with her, and Oliver, waiting patiently for her to bring some notes, gave her a considered look as she came into the office. When she dropped them all over the floor stupidly, he said nothing, only got to his feet and helped her to pick them up, nor did he comment when later that morning she muddled the children so that the wrong patient went to the first aid room. It was only at the end of the clinic, while she began to clear up and Sister Griffiths gave her a piece of her mind, that he came out of his office and asked her to give him a few minutes of her time.

She followed him inside and closed the door behind her. She had made a hash of the morning's work and she knew it without being told; all the same she apologised, and added: 'I expect you're going to give me the sack.'

'No, I'm not, Celine, but it would help if you would tell me what's the matter.' And when she didn't answer: 'Celine?' His voice was quiet, but she had to obey it.

'I'm a bit upset,' she mumbled.

'So it can be seen,' was his mild rejoinder. 'But why?' He opened a file of papers on his desk and leafed through them. 'Homesick?'

'No—oh, I miss home, how could I not? I keep thinking of the roses and the strawberries and taking Dusty for a walk . . .'

'But it's none of those things.' Oliver looked up suddenly. 'Nicky?' he asked gently.

She met his eyes honestly. 'I met him yesterday—quite by accident. I went to Green Park for most of the day and as I came out of the gates—to cross Piccadilly, you know, and look for somewhere to have my supper—he was coming along the pavement.'

She paused, expecting him to say something, but when he didn't she went on slowly, 'He told me he was getting a divorce, and he—he asked me to marry him when he was free.'

'And will you?' Oliver's voice was as placid as ever, inviting a reply.

Celine stared down at her hands, neatly folded on her lap. 'It's a funny thing,' she said slowly, 'when I was with him, it all seemed so easy and exciting, but I can't stop wondering about his wife, and I know it's silly, but I feel a bit scared of seeing him again. I said I didn't want to, but he said he'd come looking for me, and I don't think I want him to.'

Oliver's handsome head was bent over his desk and she couldn't see his face. 'There are several things we can do about that.' His voice was soothing and very reassuring. 'You can safely leave me to deal with circumstances as they arise.'

'But you may not be there.'

'Oh, but I will, Celine, just until you know your own mind.' He looked at her, smiling a little. 'And now you've got that off your chest, do you suppose you could cope a little better with the work?'

She stood up. 'Yes. I'm very sorry, I'll try, I really will. I feel better now I've told you, and I'm sorry I'm beastly to you sometimes.'

He remained serious, although his eyes gleamed.

'Try and think of me as a friend and not an interfering, middle-aged bachelor who thinks he knows everything.' He smiled then and Celine, very pink in the cheeks, managed a smile back. She looked so beautiful that the doctor went on staring at her, although he wasn't smiling any more. She wondered why. She said quickly: 'You're not middle-aged . . .'

He had pulled a folder towards him and was opening it. 'Perhaps not quite. Will you ask Maggie when you're to have your day off this week and let me know?'

Polite dismissal. She went out of the room and found Sister Griffiths. She was to have Wednesday; only one doctor would be coming in on that day and there weren't too many patients. Celine went back to the office and opened the door. Oliver was sitting just as she had left him, staring at the opposite wall, deep in thought. She said quietly: 'Sister Griffiths says Wednesday,' and when he nodded rather absently, she went out again.

Sister Griffiths might be sharp-tongued, but she didn't hold grudges. The pair of them enjoyed their snack lunch after Oliver had gone and then got ready for the afternoon's session. David Slater arrived a little early and since the waiting-room was fuller than usual, it was well past their usual closing hour by the time the last child had been seen and sent home. There wasn't an evening clinic on Mondays and Celine discovered that she was expected to give the whole place a turn-out with Mrs Thatch doing the rough work. Surprisingly she enjoyed it, and though she hadn't expected to, she fell into bed after the lavish supper Mrs Thatch had provided, and slept till morning.

The next day went well. She was getting the hang of it now, and what was more important, the patients and their mothers had accepted her. She was learning names rapidly and was no longer bewildered when Sister Griffiths told her to boil up the Spencer Wells or Oliver wanted old notes or asked her to telephone this or that hospital. And it was her day off on Wednesday; a weekday would be far more satisfactory than on Sunday; she would go to Regent Street and browse down the Burlington Arcade—she hadn't been there since she was a schoolgirl. If at the back of her mind she wondered if she would meet Nicky, she didn't allow herself to dwell on it, only she felt a vague disquiet at the idea. She supposed she would love him forever, but meeting him wasn't the answer, and in time she supposed she wouldn't feel so

bereft. Hard work certainly helped, and time—
hadn't someone said that time heals all wounds?

David Slater took the afternoon clinic, full to
overflowing, so that he stayed and had tea with
them before starting on the much smaller evening
session. He had finished and gone and Sister
Griffiths was actually going through the door
when Oliver came in.

'Still hard at work?' he wanted to know
cheerfully. 'Not going out?' And when she shook
her head, 'I thought we might spend the day
together tomorrow—I've a day off too.'

Celine stood, Vim in one hand, cleaning cloth in
the other, 'Us? A day out?'

'Why not? I'll be here at nine o'clock.' He
turned to go and she said urgently, 'Yes, but where,
and for how long?'

'Oh, here and there, you know—I've got tickets
for the theatre in the evening, and we might have
supper afterwards.'

'Oh, might we?' She knew she sounded idiotic,
but it was so unexpected.

'Why not?' He was gone. Celine stood looking
at the closed door, listening to the sound of his car
as he drove away. 'But I haven't said I'd go,' she
declared peevishly to the empty room, and then:
'What shall I wear?'

Before she went to bed that night she went
through her small wardrobe. She hadn't brought
much with her, but what there was was definitely
wearable. She decided on a dim apricot silk, the
dress with a finely pleated skirt and a plain bodice
with a white quaker collar, and its matching
jacket. A bit much for nine o'clock in the morning,
but it they were going to the theatre and to supper

afterwards, it would pass muster. And because she hadn't had the opportunity of dressing up for some time, she was up early, making a careful toilet. It was another gorgeous morning; she put on her Charles Jourdan sandals and found their matching handbag. If it rained she would be sunk, but nothing on earth would induce her to take her raincoat. She took a final look in the mirror, sprayed Femme with a lavish hand and went downstairs.

Oliver was in his office, and she had time to admire the elegance of his appearance as he glanced up, saw her, and got out of his chair.

His ' 'Morning', was casually friendly, as was his: 'You look nice. Shall we go?'

'Good morning, Oliver,' said Celine sedately. 'Where to?'

He smiled. 'A mystery tour? It's such a lovely day, would you rather drive out into the country this morning?'

'I'd like that very much, that's if you want, to?'

'I think it would be an excellent idea—Bethnal Green can be a little stifling.'

He drove out of London into Hertfordshire, not hurrying and taking the by-roads. At Much Hadham he stopped and they had coffee and buns in a small Elizabethan cottage, whose front room held a handful of tables and chairs and had a view of the charming main street. And by then Celine was enjoying herself, for Oliver was a good companion, saying very little about himself but rambling on in his placid way about this and that and never mentioning Nicky or her home and family—which for some strange reason made her eager to talk about just those things.

But he gave her no chance. Each time she turned the conversation to more personal matters, he deliberately spiked her guns. He did it nicely, but very soon she gave up; it was like banging one's head against a feather bed. They drove on presently, across Essex and into Suffolk, still by quiet country roads, to stop in Lavenham, looking, with its Tudor houses and market cross, very much as it must have done in the sixteenth century.

'Lunch?' asked Oliver, and when Celine nodded, he stopped outside the Swan Hotel, a lovely old building with beamed ceilings and a history which went back hundreds of years. Celine, healthily hungry by now, ate her way through the house pâté, wild duck stuffed with apples, vegetables to rival her home's kitchen garden and a luscious ice cream which she attacked with all the enthusiasm of a small girl.

Getting into the car presently, she said: 'I am enjoying myself.'

Oliver turned the car Londonwards. 'So am I.'

Celine didn't ask where they were going next; she was content not to know. He threaded his way through the city's heart, going towards the river, going westwards as well as south, but as they drove down the Kings Road she asked suddenly: 'Where are we going?'

'Home for tea.' And presently the car turned into a narrow road alongside the river and a row of charming old houses facing the water.

'Oh, it's Strand on the Green!' Celine turned to look at him. 'Do you know someone who lives here? Isn't it heavenly? Not like London at all.'

'I like it. I live here.'

He had drawn up before a narrow-fronted

house in the middle of the row. 'It seems a good idea to have tea here, then you can tidy up before the theatre.'

He got out and opened her door and they crossed the pavement together. Oliver opened the street door and stood aside to let her go in. The hall was narrow, panelled with white painted wood and thickly carpeted in a rich mulberry colour. It was bright and welcoming and there was a bowl of flowers on the wall table and a rather beautiful chandelier; after the spick and span austerity of the surgery it seemed like heaven to Celine.

Someone had come through the door at the end of the hall; an elderly man with a fringe of grey hair framing a round face. He was portly and dressed very precisely, and if he was surprised to see Celine his bland features gave no sign of it.

He was introduced as Pym, asked to fetch tea and show Celine to a bedroom where she might tidy herself, and tell Mrs Pym that her services might be required there. 'And you'll excuse me for a moment, Celine?' went on Oliver, all at once the doctor again. 'I've a couple of phone calls to make. Mrs Pym will take you to the sitting-room when you're ready.'

The stairs were narrow, curving gracefully to the floor above, and on the landing Celine glimpsed another small staircase and a passage leading to the back of the house before Pym opened a door and begged her to go in.

The room was small compared to her own room at home, but it was furnished in great taste with a small bed, a dressing-table under the window, a tall boy and a comfortable chair beside a drum table. The colours were muted pastels and the

carpet was white. Celine, having lived all her life
with fine furniture, looked everything over with a
knowledgeable eye and liked it very much.

She went into the adjoining bathroom, where
she washed her face and hands and did her hair,
then she made up once more, and by then Mrs
Pym had tapped on the door—a small cosy
woman who reminded her of Angela. It was very
pleasant to be fussed over again; she had begun to
get used to her spartan life at the clinic.

She accompanied Mrs Pym downstairs presently
and was ushered into a long narrow room, its
windows overlooking the river, and here the
furniture was exactly right too, a medley of
comfortable chairs and beautifully cared-for
antiques. There was no sign of Oliver. Celine went
to the window and looked out at the water,
thinking how delightful it must be to live in this
charming house. And she was surprised too. She
hadn't given Oliver much thought; he disappeared
each day in his car after the clinic was over and
she had supposed vaguely that he lived somewhere
in London—a flat, because so many people lived
in flats and they were convenient, especially for
someone on their own.

She turned round as the door opened and he
came in.

'Nice view, isn't it?' He crossed the room and
came to stand beside her. 'There's always
something to see from this window, and it's quiet.'

'It's beautiful—after Bethnal Green.' She sighed
without knowing it and he glanced down at her.

'Have you bitten off more than you can chew?'
His tone was light, but she knew him well enough
to know that he would want an answer.

'Certainly not. I found it a bit—well, strange at first, but now I like it—it's worthwhile.'

'Yes, it is.' He turned away as Pym came in with the tea tray. 'Here's tea—there's rather a nice garden behind the house, perhaps you would like to see it presently?'

They ate their tea sitting at the window— cucumber sandwiches, a rich fruit cake and tiny fairy cakes and tea from a silver pot. After Mrs Thatch's brown teapot and thick china, it was a treat. Oliver, making inroads into the cake, carried on a desultory conversation which demanded little of her attention but was just sufficient to stop her thinking too many thoughts, and presently he took her to the end of the narrow hall and opened a door into a much smaller room, a sitting-room, she supposed, although why on earth he should need two she had no idea. There was a French window here standing open and beyond it a small gravel paved patio with easy chairs and a table, and beyond that still the prettiest little garden she had ever seen. It was walled, the small old bricks almost covered by roses, a peach tree or two and clematis. The flower beds below the walls were packed with a riot of flowers and there was a very small fountain in the centre of the lawn.

'Pocket handkerchief size,' said Oliver, 'but nice to relax in when I get the time.'

'It's beautiful! Do you have a gardener? You don't look . . .' she stopped herself just in time from saying that he didn't look as though he could garden, he was too elegant.

If he noticed her hesitation he took no notice of it. 'Lord, no—I potter myself, and Pym and Mrs Pym pull the odd weed or two from time to time.

My mother had a lovely garden and I suppose I've inherited her pleasure in growing things.'

'No animals?' asked Celine.

'A battered old cat called May and couple of Jack Russells—they're at the vet's having a going over, Pym will fetch them presently.'

'I'd like to see them. And why do you call the cat May?'

'That was the month in which we found him.'

She lifted her face to the late afternoon sun. 'It must be delightful living here, but don't you wish you had more time to enjoy it?'

Oliver was standing with his hands in his pockets, leaning against the wall. 'Yes, often.' He looked as though he was going to say something else, but he didn't, and she filled an awkward little silence. 'You said we were going to the theatre—what are we going to see?'

'*Cats*—I hope you'll enjoy it, Celine.'

'Oh, I shall—it's months since I went anywhere.' She looked down at herself. 'Will I do like this?'

The glance he gave her was swift and heavy-lidded. 'Charmingly. I thought we might eat here rather earlier than usual and perhaps have supper after the show.'

'Oh, how lovely—I'd forgotten just what fun London can be!'

'But you are really a home bird, aren't you, Celine?'

'I suppose so—I mean, I could live at home and not mind very much if I never saw London again, I suppose, but if I had to live in Bethnal Green for the rest of my life, I just couldn't.'

'Could you live here?'

She answered readily, 'Of course—it's a little

oasis, isn't it? This house and garden could be anywhere—it's a perfect little world of its own.'

Oliver smiled. 'I like to think so—I'm glad you share my views.'

They dined later in a small elegant room furnished with some nice pieces of Regency mahogany, its silk-hung walls almost covered with family portraits. And Pym's wife proved herself to be just as good a cook as Angela, serving up tiny pancakes filled with mushrooms, lamb cutlets with a host of vegetables and a syllabub to follow, and there was time to sit over their coffee before leaving for the theatre. Celine, nicely full and conscious that the white Burgundy they had drunk at dinner had made her feel that the world, if not quite right, was almost so, got into the car with a small sigh of content. 'I'm having a lovely day,' she declared, and added belatedly, 'It's very kind of you—thank you very much.'

'I'm having a lovely day too.' His voice was friendly and quite impersonal.

They had excellent seats in the stalls and the theatre was full, adding to the excitement Celine felt. She sat enthralled until the interval and when Oliver suggested that they might get a drink, she got up happily and went with him to the bar.

It was crowded, and they were edging their way through the people clustered around when Oliver touched her arm. 'Over here,' he said, and a moment later: 'Hullo, Daphne.' He had stopped by a young woman, dark and attractive and strikingly dressed, who turned round to face him at once.

'Oliver, now nice to see you!' She looked at

Celine and Oliver said with a kind of lazy good humour,

'This is Celine Baylis—Celine, meet Nicky's wife, Daphne.'

Celine felt the blood draining from her face, but she had had six years of good manners drilled into her at the excellent girls' school she had been sent to—moreover, she had inherited a good deal of her father's spirit—a dreamy man now, but much decorated during the last war. She lifted her chin a very little, summoned a smile and offered a hand, her social murmur exactly right.

'Now this is nice,' exclaimed the girl. 'Mother-in-law has told me so much about you and what a great help you were while they were staying at your home. You must go and see them—Father-in-law's much better, you know.'

'Is Nicky with you?' asked Oliver idly.

She made a face. 'Yes—we're trying again, my dear. I don't suppose it'll work, but we do have to think of Mandy.' She glanced at Celine. 'My little daughter.' She looked round her. 'Heaven knows where Nicky is—go and get your drinks, Oliver, while Celine and I have a gossip.'

And when he had gone, 'I daresay you know that Nicky and I plan to separate—at least, I do; he insists on having another shot at making a go of it, but it won't work, of course. His mother and father pretend there's nothing the matter—they dote on him, although they know he wouldn't lift a finger to help them—that's left for Oliver, bless him.' She tucked a hand under Celine's elbow. 'You're very pale, is it too hot for you here?'

'It is warm,' Celine seized on the excuse, 'and I'm not used to these crushes, but I feel fine, thanks. Tell me about your little girl.'

Oliver came back with their drinks and she took hers without looking higher than his tie. She was so angry that she bubbled with rage; how dare he? He'd ruined her lovely day, and very likely he had done it deliberately. If Nicky turned up now she wasn't sure what she would do. But he didn't; Oliver took them both back presently and left Daphne in her seat before they settled once more in their own. But now all the fun had gone out of the evening. Celine hardly heard a note and the stage was a meaningless blur. She couldn't wait for it all to end, and when finally it was over and they stood up and began the slow progress to the exit, she saw Daphne waving. She waved back, sick at heart to see Nicky beside her. He hadn't wanted even to meet her, and a good thing too—she didn't know who she hated most, him or his massive cousin, behaving for all the world as though nothing was the matter!

They had to walk a little way to the car, and neither spoke until they were in it. As he drove away from the theatre she exploded. 'You knew—you knew, didn't you? That they were going to be there. You did it deliberately—you've spoilt my lovely day . . .' She stopped because she was going to cry, the last thing she wanted to do, especially in front of him.

Oliver slid the car into the stream of traffic leaving the theatre.

His, 'Yes, I did it deliberately, Celine,' was imperturbable.

'I want to go back to the surgery,' muttered Celine. 'I don't want to go out to supper with you, now or ever—I don't want to see you again ever!'

She was aware that this was a very unfair remark and that it would be difficult to adhere to. She added fiercely: 'Nicky said you always interfered...'

'Tell me something,' asked Oliver, at his most placid, ignoring her tears and sniffs. 'Did you intend seeing Nicky again? Willingly?'

'Of course not!'

'You are in fact crying for the moon. Far more sense if you looked up at your star—your midsummer star, remember?'

She didn't answer that. By the time he drew up before the surgery door she had stopped crying and had mopped her face and was staring stonily in front of her.

Oliver was out of the car and opening her door before she could do anything about it. He opened the surgery door too and stood aside to let her go in, then followed her. Mrs Thatch had left a light on in the hall and there was a note propped up against the flowers on the table, addressed to Celine.

She picked it up and saw that the writing was Nicky's, hardly noticing Oliver's sharp glance as he passed her on his way to the little kitchen.

She opened it slowly and felt sick as she read it: Nicky had called to see her, he had splendid news and he begged her to see him again. His wife had left him, he would be free in a few months, he was her devoted Nicky.

She stood with the letter dangling from one hand. She didn't want to cry any more, only run away and hide somewhere. Oliver came back and took the letter from her without asking, read it and then tore it very deliberately in pieces. 'There's a nice pot of tea waiting,' he told her, and propelled her into the kitchen and on to a chair. Apparently unnoticing of her dead white face and shaking hands, he perched on the edge of the table and said cheerfully, 'I've got a job for you tomorrow. There's a Mrs Hawkins living in Sunshine Row who's being unco-operative about bringing her young Linda to see me. The child was in hospital for weeks with Huntington's chorea, her mum took her home before she should have been discharged and although we've sent follow-up letters, there's no trace. I want you to go and see her if you can and persuade her that it's vital to Linda's health that she should come here. I'll leave the address and the particulars on my desk so you can go after breakfast. If you find a situation you can't cope with, ring back here—I'll leave a note for David.' He didn't ask if she wanted to go, he had taken it for granted that she would do as she was told. 'Have you any idea what chorea is?'

She said slowly: 'Wasn't it called St Vitus' Dance years ago?'

'Near enough. Use your eyes while you're there, make sure Linda's being cared for as far as possible, and above all, try and get Mrs Hawkins to bring her here.' He stretched out an arm and took the mug from her hand. 'Now go to bed.'

Celine got up obediently and he stood up too. Whatever she felt, manners had to be remembered. She said in a rigid voice: 'Thank you for my day out,' and then, the manners forgotten, hurled herself at him and buried her head against his shoulder. She was a big girl; it was fortunate that he was an even bigger man. He caught her deftly and held her close while she grizzled. Presently she pulled away and raised her eyes to his. 'I must be mad,' she told him, 'after what you did this evening.' She drew a deep breath and then rushed on in a rather loud voice, 'I said I didn't want to see you ever again, and I meant it!'

'That's a perfectly natural reaction.' Oliver opened the door for her. 'Don't forget Mrs Hawkins in the morning, will you?'

She brushed past him with a muttered goodnight and once in her room tore off her clothes and jumped into bed. She wouldn't sleep, of that she was certain; her head was seething with odds and ends of thoughts which needed sorting out before morning. 'Nicky, oh, Nicky!' she said to the dark room, but it was Oliver's calm face which her mind's eye saw before she fell into exhausted, dreamless sleep.

CHAPTER SIX

IT was a dull morning when she woke, but warm. She found Sister Griffiths already in the surgery when she went down after her breakfast, and that lady lost no time in telling her to be off to Sunshine Row. 'We've all tried our luck with Mrs Hawkins, perhaps you'll do better. Be sure and telephone if you're worried about anything.'

Sunshine Row didn't live up to its name. Even on the brightest of days it would have been gloomy, and now, under a steady drizzle from a grey sky, it looked the very antithesis of that name. It was a narrow lane, with a high brick wall, surrounding some nameless factory running its length on one side, and a row of mean little houses on the other. The pavement was greasy, and old plastic bags, cigarette cartons, banana skins and orange peel made walking on it hazardous. Her instructions said number six; Celine knocked on the half-open door and when a harsh voice bade her come in, she went. The hall was narrow with threadbare lino on the floor and it smelled of onions and cabbage and washing. Guided by the voice, she went upstairs and came face to face with a sharp-featured woman with her hair in curlers, swathed in a grubby overall.

'Mrs Hawkins?' asked Celine in what she hoped was a confident voice.

'S'right. 'Oo are you?' The woman jerked her head. 'If you're from Security you can 'op it—spying on me!'

'I'm from Dr Seymour.' Celine was relieved to see the woman's face soften a little, although her voice was harsh still.

''E wants to see little Linda, does 'e? Well, tell 'im from me that she's O.K. 'E did 'er a lot of good in 'orspital, but 'ome's where she belongs.'

'I'm sure he agrees with you,' said Celine hastily. 'It's just that if he could keep an eye on her each week, there'd never be any need for her to go into hospital. Perhaps no one explained that to you? And I'm sure he'd arrange for Linda to be taken to the surgery with you.'

''Ow d'yer mean, a taxi?'

Celine crossed her fingers. 'That's right, he asked me to fix things if you would agree.'

'No strings?'

'None. He—or his partner—just want to take a look at Linda at regular intervals.'

Mrs Hawkins stared hard at her. 'Come on in,' she invited.

The room was clean but crowded with furniture and with a line of washing hanging above their heads. There was a small balcony at one end and two more doors—kitchen and bathroom, guessed Celine, and saw the bed in one corner with a child, presumably Linda, on it. She was a very small girl, thin and feverish-looking, and Celine's soft heart ached at the sight of her. 'Is she your only one?' she asked gently.

'Only one alive,' said Mrs Hawkins matter-of-factly. 'Me 'usband's dead too.'

'Does Dr Seymour know that?'

'Course not—'e only died a month ago.' She gave Celine a pitying look. 'New around 'ere, ain't yer?'

'Yes, I am, Mrs Hawkins. Would you tell me when it would be convenient for you to be fetched with Linda and I'll ask Dr Seymour to arrange it.'

Mrs Hawkins shrugged. 'Termorrer. Mind you, I can't afford ter pay.'

'I'm sure he'll understand that—indeed, he asked me to find out if you needed anything for Linda.' Celine told the lie quite convincingly: 'He gave me some money . . .'

'A real gent. 'Elped me when Linda was ill, 'e did, told me to ask 'im if I needed anything, but I've got me pride, see, and Jim was alive then.'

'Yes, of course, but you're on your own now.' Celine opened her purse and took out a five-pound note. 'It's not charity, Mrs Hawkins, it's to help Linda to get well.'

She walked back quickly, oblivious of the rain. She must see Oliver and tell him and ask him to do something to help Mrs Hawkins and that pitiful scrap staring at her from the bed in the corner.

The clinic was only half over, and there was no one free to tell; she waited until the last patient had gone and because Sister Griffiths was busy writing, went along to Oliver's room.

He wasn't there. David Slater sat in his chair, tidying his notes. He looked up with a smile as Celine went in and asked: 'Any luck?'

'Yes, I think so. I—expected to see Dr Seymour . . .'

'Oh, he's away for a few days, but he told me about Mrs Hawkins,' he scrabbled round among the papers on the desk—'there's a note somewhere.'

Celine was aware of bitter disappointment. She had for the moment forgotten that she never wanted to see Oliver again. Just now he was the one person she did want to see, but David Slater would have to do instead.

She explained at some length and he listened carefully. When she had finished he said: 'You've done very well—I'll make a note of that fiver and let you have it back. Get Sister Griffiths to arrange a taxi for tomorrow morning, will you?'

'Could you let Dr Seymour know?'

David Slater gave her a quick look of surprise. 'Well, I don't suppose he wants to be disturbed when he's on holiday.'

She agreed in a subdued voice, 'No, of course not—how silly of me!'

She went back to her chores. Oliver hadn't said a word about going on holiday, but then why should he? He never talked about himself, even when they had been together all day. She couldn't remember his telling her anything relating to his private life. But then why should he have done? She had shown clearly enough that she wasn't in the least interested. She had been appallingly rude too, thinking about it made her blush hotly; she would apologise when she saw him again. For some reason she felt depressed for the rest of the day, and it wasn't because of Nicky. To her surprise she discovered, by the end of the evening session, that she hadn't given him so much as one thought. On the other hand, she had been wondering frequently what Oliver was doing and where he had gone.

Her spirits were still low after supper. She went downstairs to the office and telephoned her mother, to be told by her that the bed and breakfast business was flourishing, that Dusty missed her, and when was she coming home for a day or two?

'I hope Oliver isn't working you too hard,' observed her mother's voice anxiously, and when Celine reassured her: 'Well, of course, he's far too nice to do that. Have you bought anything nice, darling?'

It was a little difficult to make her mother understand that she didn't have a great deal of time to go shopping. Free time was limited and it was quite a journey to Harrods or the smart little boutiques around Sloane Street. Her mother said comfortably: 'Oh, well, darling, I daresay Oliver would give you a lift if you asked him.'

It seemed unlikely to Celine that Oliver would ever offer to take her anywhere again. Between weeping all over him and calling him names she had proved herself to be a companion any man in his right mind would shun. She rang off presently, feeling she wasn't needed anywhere; Aunt Chloe was managing splendidly, and Nurse Byng would be coming back from her holiday on Friday, and it would be quite possible to manage without her amateurish efforts at the surgery.

The week wore on slowly, the only bright spot being the arrival of Mrs Hawkins and Linda and that lady's promise that provided she had a taxi she would attend regularly.

'Nice enough,' she confided to Celine, on her way out, 'that young doctor, but not a patch on Dr Seymour. I wish 'e was 'ere.'

Celine, rather more grammatically wished he was too.

On Thursday evening Sister Griffiths announced that she would be going on holiday herself on Saturday for a week, and Celine would find Dorothy Byng very easy to get on with. 'And when I get back you shall have your weekend,' she promised. 'And I must say you've earned it; when I first saw you I never thought you'd stick it, but you have, and you're a real help to all of us.' She added as an afterthought: 'You're far too pretty, of course.'

Celine went pink. 'Why, thank you, Sister Griffiths . . .'

'And you might as well call me Maggie, everyone else does.'

Nurse Byng worked part-time, but when Sister Griffiths was away, she came for the whole day. She was a short stout woman with a round cheerful face and a tremendous capacity for hard work, and although she lacked Sister Griffiths' severity, she conformed to that lady's high standards. But she did enjoy a good gossip; from her Celine learned that David Slater was married to a French girl and had a baby daughter to whom Dr Seymour was godfather. 'And if you ask me,' added Nurse Byng, 'he ought to marry himself and have a family of his own. It's a waste, a nice man like him being single. He had an unhappy affair years ago and it turned him off women—at least that's what they say. Always the gentleman, mind you, but never meets the right girl, though heaven knows he's had plenty of girl-friends. Of course, he's got family commitments, and that good-for-nothing cousin of his does his best to make trouble.'

'What sort of commitments?' asked Celine, anxious to know more.

'Well, he's the one with the money—lent any amount to that cousin and for all I know never had a penny of it back.' She darted a look at Celine, sitting composedly eating her lunch. 'You met his uncle and aunt, didn't you?'

'Yes. They were nice.'

'That son of theirs costs them a packet, by all accounts. He's got a nice little wife too—and a child. Some men never know when to settle down, do they?'

'It seems not,' murmured Celine. Nicky somehow seemed unimportant now. She supposed she had loved him, but that love was so dead now she couldn't remember how she had felt, only a blessed relief that she no longer thought about him or cared in the least what happened to him. Oliver had been right, and it would be her just desserts if he were to say, I told you so. She poured more coffee and reflected that she wouldn't mind if he did just so long as he was there to say something. The surgery seemed very empty without him.

In two days' time it would be Sunday, and she had made no plans, refusing to admit to herself that she was nervous of running into Nicky. There had been nothing since the note Oliver had torn up in such a high-handed manner, and perhaps he would never try to contact her again, she hoped so. But she would have to get out, away from the surgery—out of London.

Her problem was solved for her by Dorothy Byng, who during the course of the evening clinic wanted to know if she would like to spend Sunday afternoon with her. 'We live at Greenwich, just me and Bill and Emma—that's our daughter. It's an easy trip once you know the way, just through the Blackwall Tunnel—the bus takes you almost to the door, but Bill will come for you—about two o'clock. We can have a walk in the park and you must stay to supper.'

'Won't I be a nuisance?' protested Celine. 'I mean, you don't get much time at home . . .'

'Bless you, Celine, it'll be a treat to have you. You can talk clothes with Emma—she's fourteen and mad about fashion, and Bill likes a chat with someone different.'

'Well, if you're sure I won't be in the way, I'd love to come.' Celine beamed with pleasure and relief. 'And you're awfully kind to ask me.'

Saturday didn't seem so bad now that she had something to look forward to on Sunday. She washed her hair, washed her smalls, did some ironing and her nails, accompanied Mrs Thatch on a shopping expedition to the local shops and went to bed early with a book; not an exciting day, but as she reminded herself, next weekend she would be home.

She enjoyed her Sunday outing too. Bill, a short taciturn man with a nice smile, drove her to Greenwich, to the small terraced house where Dorothy welcomed her with a warmth which made up for her rather lonely weekend. They went for a walk almost as soon as she arrived, with Emma hanging on her arm, eagerly talking about clothes. 'That's a lovely dress,' she declared, eyeing Celine's Italian jersey dress with frank envy. 'I'll have those sort of clothes when I'm older.'

'They last for years,' said Celine practically. 'They're more expensive to buy, but they go on and on. What are you going to do when you leave school?'

They went back for a large, old-fashioned tea presently, cake and scones and jam and a plate of bread and butter, and Celine was allowed to help with the washing up while Bill watched the news on T.V. They just sat and talked after that, and Celine found herself trying to lead the talk round to Oliver, but Dorothy at home wasn't as gossipy as she was at the surgery. She gave up presently and went round the house with her hostess, admiring everything they had done to improve it. They were a happy family, that was evident, and Celine, who had been feeling unaccountably disturbed about something she couldn't place a finger on, felt soothed by that.

They sat down to supper presently—cold ham and salad and pickles and a gorgeous trifle washed down by cups of coffee. She got up to go with real reluctance, not wanting to end her day.

'You must come again,' said Dorothy kindly,

'and next time we go shopping for Emma, perhaps you'd come with us—to give us advice, you know. She knows what she wants, but sometimes it goes wrong.'

'Oh, I'd love to. We could go to Laura Ashley—not expensive, and caters for Emma's age group.'

Celine said goodbye and see you tomorrow, then got into the little car beside Bill, still taciturn but friendly as he drove her back to Bethnal Green.

'Nice to have had you,' he told her on parting. 'And our Emma's taken to you—you must come again.'

She thanked him and meant it when she said that she would like to. She unlocked the door and went in with a last wave as she shut the door behind her.

There was a letter for her on the hall table. She knew the handwriting, of course, and just for a moment she was tempted to tear it to pieces, but curiosity got the better of her good judgement, and she opened it. Nicky had called, it said, he wanted to see her and why hadn't she answered his last letter. He would explain everything.

Celine read it to the end, put it back in the envelope and went upstairs to bed, wishing with all her heart that Oliver had been there to tear it into tiny pieces with casual contempt. She didn't do that, but laid it on the dressing-table and got ready for bed, where, surprisingly enough, she forgot all about it, her head fully occupied with speculation as to when Oliver would return.

The surgery was always busy on a Monday morning. The waiting-room was already comfortably full as she went through it on her way to the office with the post. There was still fifteen minutes before Dr Slater would arrive, and Dorothy had warned her that she might be a little late if the traffic was heavy. Celine opened the office door and went in briskly, to stop short at the sight of Oliver sitting at his desk. He looked elegant, too elegant for his surroundings, but probably he was going on later that morning to his hospital rounds or whatever he did—she was a bit vague about that.

She said breathlessly: 'Oh, Oliver, how nice to see you . . .' but anything else she had been going to say was choked back because of his raised eyebrows and the amused surprise on his face. She remembered then that she had told him that she never wanted to see him again, and he'd remembered that too. She stuck out her beautiful chin. 'Good morning,' and she put the post on the desk and turned to go.

His pleasant, 'Good morning, Celine,' made her hesitate and she turned right round again when he went on, still very pleasant, but distant too: 'Let me introduce Dr Peter Trent—he's to be the third partner here. Peter, this is Miss Celine Baylis, our—er—right hand around the place.'

She hadn't noticed him because she had had eyes only for Oliver, but now she looked at the young man standing in a corner of the office. He was a little above middle height and slim, with a shock of fair hair and bright blue eyes in a face which just missed good looks. They shook hands and Celine, returning his smile, thought he looked nice, and certainly more friendly than Oliver.

'Nurse Byng here?' asked Oliver. 'If she is, will you ask her to come in?'

She said, 'Yes, Dr Seymour,' in what she hoped sounded like a coolly efficient voice, and whisked out of the room and bumped, luckily enough, into Dorothy's cosy person.

'He's back,' said Celine. 'He wants you in the office.'

Nurse Byng nodded, her sharp eyes on Celine's face. 'There's a child feeling sick—will you deal with him?'

Celine did her best. She was still somewhat inept but she was willing and patient and outwardly serene; inside she blazed at the cool way Oliver had dismissed her, and presently the blaze turned into a kind of sadness. She was only just beginning to realise what a dependable man he was, and undemanding too. No wonder his aunt and uncle had sent for him—and she had treated him very badly. She would have to apologise and hope they would be friends again. Performing her mundane tasks, she tried out several speeches, not too eager, she hoped, but extending a whole bouquet of olive branches if he should choose to grasp it. The clinic was almost over, she would catch him before he left.

She was speeding the last small patient on his way when Oliver went past her, got into his car and drove off. He wouldn't be back until the evening, Dorothy Byng told her over their hasty lunch. David Slater would be coming for the afternoon clinic—a small one, as it happened, and the new doctor would stay all day. 'Doctor Seymour seems anxious to work him in as quickly as possible,' said Dorothy. 'Perhaps he's planning to do fewer hours here—I wouldn't be surprised. He's got a big practice, you know, as well as beds in several hospitals. He's very high up in his profession—internationally well-known, one might say.' She passed her cup for more coffee. 'We'd better get a move on. The new man's nice, but he is a bit slow.'

It was strange, but Celine was quite unable to speak to Oliver alone. He came and went, and it always seemed to her that he did this just at the very moment when she was too busy to get to the office. It was Saturday morning and Sister Griffiths was back, refreshed from her holiday and more exacting than ever, before she was told she was to have her weekend. 'Though you'll have to stay until the morning clinic's over this morning,' said Sister Griffiths, 'because Nurse Byng has to take her daughter to the dentist, and won't be coming in. You can have an extra half day to make up for that later on.'

Celine thanked her. It was short notice with a vengeance, but it would take only a couple of minutes to fling some things into an overnight bag and get a bus to Paddington. She had no idea of the trains ... something that didn't matter, as it turned out, because young Dr Peter Trent waylaid her between the waiting room and the surgery and asked her in a bumbling fashion if he could give her a lift.

'I'm going down to Bath for the weekend, and it's not at all out of my way,' he explained, 'and I've got to be back here on Monday morning. I'd give you a lift back on Sunday evening—it's really no trouble.'

Celine beamed at him. 'I'd be very grateful— I've been wondering about trains and things. Are you going from here at the end of the clinic?'

He nodded. 'I've got my case in the car—I don't suppose you'd take long to pack?'

'Five minutes—ten at the most. And thank you very much, Dr Trent.'

'Everyone calls you Celine,' he mumbled, 'perhaps you'd call me Peter?'

'All right, Peter. I'll be as quick as I can. Are you sure it's no trouble?'

He shook his head. 'It'll be nice to have company.'

He went into the surgery, and a few minutes later Oliver arrived and the stream of patients started to ooze slowly from the waiting-room to the office.

Half way through the session Oliver looked up from his desk. He asked casually: 'Did Celine agree to your offer of a lift home, Peter?'

'Yes, I think she was jolly pleased about it— saves her a lot of fussing about with trains and so on. It was kind of you to suggest it—thank you, sir.'

Oliver picked up the next batch of notes. 'It's a long drive on your own,' he observed laconically. 'Now this next child . . .'

The moment the door had shut on the last of the patients, Sister Griffiths shooed Celine away. 'Go and get your things together before we change our minds,' she counselled.

'Yes, but I wanted to see Dr Seymour about something . . .'

'Well, you can't,' declared Sister Griffiths forthrightly. 'He told me I was to go in the moment surgery was over, and he won't thank you for changing his plans. Off with you, and have a good time.'

So Celine nipped up to her room, crammed a few odds and ends into her overnight bag and raced downstairs again, to find Peter Trent waiting at the wheel of his little Triumph sports car. She had found time to change into the Italian knitted dress, and he eyed her with open admiration and a touch of wonder as to why a girl who dressed as she did and tossed a Gucci bag into the back of the car as though it were something from Woolworth's should earn her living slaving in a surgery in Bethnal Green. After all, she wasn't even a nurse, and some of the work she had to do was pretty grisly.

'I thought we might stop on the way and have a bite to eat at a pub,' he told her as he shot off down the street. Oliver watched them go.

It was a pleasant trip. Peter might have admired her openly, but that was all. They were soon chatting like old friends, and when eventually they arrived at her home, he came in with her, met her parents and Aunt Chloe, and stayed for an early tea.

'There's a nice boy,' observed Mrs Baylis approvingly. 'A bit young . . .' She threw a quick glance at Celine's face. 'He is going to drive you back, dear?' And when Celine said that yes, he was, her mother went on: 'How kind! I was so sorry to hear from Oliver that he couldn't bring you down himself. He came down to see us—oh, a few days ago—no, longer than that,' she mused vaguely, 'and he told us that he'd be driving you down and would stay the weekend here. I wonder what changed his plans?'

Celine heard the query in her mother's innocent voice. 'He's a very busy man,' she said stonily.

Her mother appeared not to notice the stoniness. 'Well, he is an important person, I suppose, in his own field—lots of consulting work—it must take him everywhere. He said how hard you worked.' Her mother hesitated. 'Has it helped, darling?'

Celine took her mother's arm. 'Yes, Mother, it has. Nicky doesn't mean anything anymore—did Oliver tell you that I'd met him by accident? Well, at first I thought how marvellous to see him again, but of course it wasn't, and I met his wife—she's nice. Did you know he had a little girl?'

'Dear me, how very odd that he never mentioned that, but now you've got over him, Celine, I must admit that neither your father nor I really took to him.' She added guilelessly, 'This Peter is much nicer.'

'He's very young, Mother.'

'Two years older than you, darling.'

Celine laughed a little. 'You know, I feel at least ten years older than I really am, it must be all the hard work. Now tell me how things are going here—are you really doing well, and is Aunt Chloe quite happy? I can always come home . . .'

'No need,' Mrs Baylis spoke hastily. 'We're really doing very well. I had no idea there were so many people wanting bed and breakfast, and people are beginning to recommend us, too. Aunt Chloe is in her element, too . . . no, love, there's no need for you to come home just yet. London must be quite fun, and you need a change from the country.'

Celine didn't disillusion her. She thought it likely that her mother hadn't the least idea what her work entailed or where exactly the surgery was. She enlarged on the lighter aspects of her job, described in detail Oliver's house and the pleasant day they had had together, and forbore from mentioning Mrs Hawkins and Linda and how often the small patients were sick all over the place and who it was who cleared up the mess. Thinking about it, she was surprised to discover that she no longer minded doing that, it was all part and parcel of the day's job, and if Oliver could mop up an ailing child without turning a hair, then she could too.

The weekend went swiftly and she enjoyed every minute of it. The house was full, and she helped when and where she could and spent as much time as she could in the garden. Barney and Angela and old Bennett had welcomed her back with delight, and Dusty had gone mad in an elderly sort of way. She got up early in the morning and took him for a walk, wishing, without going too deeply into it, that Oliver had been there too. And when Sunday evening came all too soon, she said goodbye with regret, at the same time aware that she was looking forward to seeing Oliver again.

Peter was full of his own weekend and anxious to talk about it. There was, he told her cautiously in case she laughed, a girl—the daughter of a neighbouring farmer who lived just outside Bath—she was eighteen and pretty: 'Though not half as pretty as you,' he added with youthful candour.

'I daresay she's prettier,' declared Celine kindly, 'only different to look at. Is she dark or fair?'

The time passed very pleasantly, and as they began the slow drive through the city, she found the excitement inside her mounting. 'It'll be nice to get back to work,' she said happily, aware that

that wasn't quite what she meant.

The surgery looked dreary in the dreary street, but once inside, that was all changed. Mrs Thatch had left a light on in the hall and there was a big pot of red geraniums on the table. Celine had said goodbye to Peter and gone inside quickly. It was getting on for ten o'clock and a cup of tea and bed were indicated. But in the hall she paused. There was a message on the pad by the telephone with her name printed above it. Would she ring Nicky when she came in, never mind how late, and below that message Oliver had written in his large forceful hand: 'Don't telephone, wait until you see me in the morning.'

Celine tore the sheet off the pad and ignoring the message read his words again. It was exactly the kind of thing he would do, she thought, and really she was old enough to do as she pleased. But underneath this thought a small voice reminded her that she didn't want to see Nicky again or hear from him—indeed, he was beginning to make her uneasy with his persistence. Was he hoping to convince her that he loved her?

She went slowly upstairs and found Mrs Thatch waiting for her with a tray of tea and a plate of sandwiches, and a very natural desire to know what sort of a weekend she'd had. It was half an hour or more before Celine gained her own room, and by then she was too tired to telephone anyone, even if she'd wanted to.

Monday morning's clinic was always a busy one. She was dealing with the first of the patients when Oliver came in, wished her good morning in passing and then apparently forgot about her. True, she fetched and carried for him and David, but with no time to say a word, and Sister Griffiths, although pleased to see her, wasn't one to allow slacking. Olive went towards the end of the morning, leaving his partner to finish, and Celine and Sister Griffiths gobbled their lunch and got ready for the afternoon session, mercifully a short one.

Oliver returned towards its close and as Celine was handing the last baby to its mother he came into the waiting room.

'We'll have our little talk now,' he told her unsmilingly, and she followed him meekly into the office and sat down in the chair he offered her.

'A pleasant weekend?' he asked in the distantly pleasant voice she didn't like very much.

'Yes, thank you. Mother said . . . she said you'd intended spending the weekend there.'

'In the light of past circumstances, hardly a good idea.' His voice was smooth and he didn't smile. Celine sat still and waited, but he didn't say anything, and after a few moments she realised he was actually waiting for her to speak. And now that the opportunity had come, she couldn't remember a single word of her prepared speeches. Instead she blurted out: 'I'm so ashamed—I've been beastly to you and so rude, and the silly thing is, I don't—didn't mean a word of it. You've been so kind, I don't quite know what I should have done without your friendship—something foolish, I daresay. I hope you'll forgive me.' She looked at him then and saw that he was still unsmiling, and she got a little frightened. 'I do mean that,' she told him urgently. 'I said I never wanted to see you again, but it was a silly lie. I—I was quite glad to come back . . .'

'To work?' His voice was very quiet.

'No, to see you. You're the nicest friend I've ever had.'

'Thank you, Celine.' He got up and came to stand in front of her. 'Shall we shake hands on that?' And then: 'Now this matter of Nicky. I'm afraid he's not going to leave you alone, you know. He's conceited, you see, and finds it difficult to realise that not everyone falls in love with him and stays that way.' He watched the colour stream into Celine's cheeks. 'There have been other girls,' he observed gently. 'Does he bother you?'

'Yes—I'm scared of meeting him again. Isn't that silly? Not because I'm afraid of him, just—well, I feel silly and ashamed.'

'You have no need to feel either. We've all fallen in and out of love at some time or another. There is a way by which he could be discouraged, probably for good . . .' He broke off as Sister Griffiths came in.

'There's a child coming in shortly—a small boy, lives in the next street. A neighbour just called in—he's that diabetic we couldn't stabilise. His mum wouldn't wait for anyone to go round.'

'Thomas Cribb,' said Oliver instantly. 'He'll have to be admitted again, but we'd better work on him here first.'

He got up to follow Sister Griffiths out of the room and Celine got up too. 'Be ready to make tea for his mum, Celine, and you'll probably have to ring for the ambulance and warn the hospital—I'll let you know.'

He paused at the door. 'A propos, Nicky—we could get engaged.'

Celine goggled at his retreating back, looking

like a very beautiful stranded fish, not sure that she had heard him aright, and then, quite sure that she had, only the commotion as the little boy was brought in penetrated her utter amazement and sent her scuttling to put on the kettle.

CHAPTER SEVEN

FOR the next hour Celine was kept busy doing the odd jobs no one else had the time to do, while Oliver and Maggie used their combined skills on small Thomas.

One of her most difficult tasks had been to find out from his mother exactly what had happened. She had told Oliver that Thomas had eaten sweeties and on the strength of that he had set to work on the semi-conscious child, telling Celine to get as many details as quickly as possible. But Mum was rendered more or less speechless by fright and tears, and it had taken a strong cup of tea and all Celine's patience to extract information. Barley sugar, she managed finally; his granny had thought it such a shame that the other children could have the sweeties she had brought them, and poor little Thomas wasn't allowed them. He had had just one, and because he had liked it so much, she had given him another and then another. Celine relayed this to Oliver, who listened with an impassive face and no hint of censure.

'We'll do our best,' he told her kindly. 'Thomas will have to go into hospital and stay for some time until he's stabilised again.'

And when finally Thomas was fit to be moved and the ambulance was on the way, his mother burst into tears once more and declared herself quite incapable of accompanying him, so that Celine found herself in the ambulance too, terrified that Thomas would do something sudden and utterly incomprehensible to her; she felt a bit better when the second ambulance man got in with them; a pleasant middle-aged man who didn't seem to be in the least worried. She clutched the papers Oliver had given her with instructions to hand them over to the Ward Sister and no one else, and was thankful that the journey was a short one.

The hospital was large, modernised here and there and full of bewildering passages. Celine followed the trolley up to the children's ward, handed over the papers to Sister, answered a few questions as well as she could and prepared to leave. Thomas, still only half awake, clung to her hand and looked scared, but he was easily persuaded to transfer his attention to a motherly nurse who called him ducky and promised him an orange if he was a good boy. Celine couldn't find Sister, she had disappeared, and the nurses she met all looked far too busy to tell her how to get out of the place. There were little signs on the walls here and there, though, and by dint of following these she found herself at the front entrance.

Her sigh of relief turned to a gasp when she realised that she had no money with her. There were plenty of buses she could have taken too—it would have to be a taxi, and she could pay when they got back to the surgery. Only there were no taxis to be seen; she waited for five minutes and then decided that she would have to walk. She wasn't at all sure of the way, but she had a tongue in her head. She stepped off the pavement and a car skidded to a halt beside her.

'Get in,' said Oliver as he got out. 'I'll be about ten minutes.' He had gone before she could say a word.

He was a little more than that, but Celine didn't mind; she was tired with all the excitement and closed her eyes, oblivious of the rush and noise of the traffic. But she woke up when Oliver got in beside her; there was so much of him that he took up all his own seat and crowded her out as well.

'He'll do,' he said briefly, and turned the car into the traffic.

Celine, very conscious of their last conversation, racked her brains for an impersonal topic, but Oliver, beyond those two brief words, seemed to have forgotten that she was there, so she sat silent, wondering if she had dreamed it all. And then when they arrived back at the surgery and he said matter-of-factly: 'Maggie will have tea waiting— get a cup and give her a hand, will you?' she was sure she had.

In any case, there was no time to bother about it. The clinic wasn't a large one but full of little annoyances and setbacks. By the end of it, Celine was finding it difficult to keep her temper, and she could tell by Maggie's pursed-up mouth that she was feeling fed up too. But finally the waiting-room was empty and they began clearing up. They had almost finished when Maggie's husband arrived.

'Thought I'd give you a treat and drive you home,' he explained cheerfully, and when Maggie demurred because there were still one or two jobs to do Celine bustled her off. 'I've got all the evening,' she declared, 'and I'm not going out.'

She was ready in another ten minutes and switched off the lights and started for the stairs. There was no sign of Oliver, but he must have left while she was in the first aid room at the back. Just as well, she thought, after that astonishing remark. A joke, she finally decided.

'We'll go out for a meal,' said Oliver from the foot of the stairs. 'Can you be ready in fifteen minutes? I've a couple of phone calls to make.' He was staring up at her rather intently, but his voice was as placid as ever.

'Me?' asked Celine stupidly, suddenly shy of being with him. 'I was going to have supper . . .'

'So was I—we might just as well have it together. Besides, we must finish our talk.' He turned away. 'Fifteen minutes, then.'

'I shall be at least twenty minutes,' said Celine haughtily, and was instantly terrified that he wouldn't take her out after all.

She heard him chuckle as she opened her door.

It would have to be the Italian dress again. She would really have to bring back some more clothes next time she went home. She showered and did her face and hair and dressed, and still having five minutes to spare, sat down and tried to bring some order to her thoughts, but five minutes wasn't enough, and she was just as muddled as she went down the stairs, to find Oliver sitting on the bottom step reading the evening paper.

She would never know until the day she died what made her so sure and so suddenly aware that she was in love with him. Perhaps it was the sight of his broad back, bowed over the paper, or the way he had put it down and got to his feet and smiled at her. It didn't really matter anyway, because it was inevitable, she knew that in her very bones; had known it for weeks and not recognised it. Now she glowed with delight, so chock-a-block with love that Oliver's impassive face, showing no more than a friendly smile, made it impossible for the moment to accept the obvious fact that whatever her own feelings, he didn't share them.

She didn't trust herself to speak, but he didn't appear to notice. 'There's a nice place I thought we might go to—A l'Ecu de France—I've booked a table. I'll have to a take a quick look at Thomas on the way, but that shouldn't take too long. I hope you're famished—I am.'

Celine had had time to pull herself together. 'I'm always starving—there's quite a lot of me to keep going.'

He opened the door for her. 'And all of it very nice,' she heard him observe.

It seemed better to ignore that. 'It's been quite a busy day,' she said in what she hoped sounded a casual voice.

They didn't talk much. Oliver left her for five minutes while he went into the hospital, and when he returned it was Thomas who supplied the matter for conversation. Almost recovered, declared Oliver with satisfaction, but it had been touch and go. 'I'll go round and see his Mum tomorrow,' he said. 'There should be time, Peter and David will be at the surgery.' He took her by surprise by changing the subject rapidly. 'Did you have a good weekend? Peter's a nice lad?'

'Delightful, thank you, and yes, Peter is nice, but very young.'

'Older than you, Celine.' That was what her mother had said.

The restaurant was charming and they had a table in a corner so that they could talk undisturbed. Not that Celine wanted that. Now that the opportunity had occurred, she wanted to put it off; her head was full of excited thoughts, continuously damped down by his casual friendly manner. But first there was the important question of what they should eat.

'Smoked salmon?' suggested Oliver, 'and what about Boeuf Stroganoff to follow? Or perhaps you'd prefer fish?'

Celine settled for the beef, accepted a glass of sherry and hoped silently that Oliver had forgotten that he was going to finish their little talk. And it seemed that he had; she had polished off the salmon and was making inroads into the beef when he suddenly switched from desultory talk. 'Ah yes, Celine—we have to discuss this question of getting engaged.' He uttered this remark in the most prosaic of tones, and she paled a little. To have a proposal from a man she was madly in love with and to know that he didn't mean a word of it was tearing her apart. But on no account must he know that. She said in a calm little voice,

'You were joking . . .'

He looked surprised. 'Good lord, no! It's the only answer, isn't it? If Nicky thinks I'm going to marry you, he'll drop you like a hot brick.'

'Why?'

'A number of reasons we don't need to go into.'

'You mean just pretend to be engaged until he's

found another girl, or gone off me?'

Oliver's mouth twitched. 'Exactly so. It shouldn't take long,' he added kindly. 'We shall have to spend some time in each other's company, of course, visit my aunt and uncle and allow ourselves to be seen around—we have a number of mutual acquaintances.'

'I'll have to tell Mother and Father.'

'I'm sure they'll approve.'

The waiter took their plates and offered the menu. 'Do you like the sound of pancakes filled with raspberries and cream, or a sorbet perhaps?'

'The pancakes, please. Why should they approve?' Celine heard her voice, nicely controlled, but if this conversation went on much longer she rather thought she might do something ghastly, like bursting into tears.

'I'm sure they wouldn't like the idea of you being pestered.'

'I don't like being pestered either,' she told him with a touch of asperity. She really was on the verge of tears, any moment now she was going to panic.

'That's settled, then. You'll go on working at the clinic, of course?'

'If you'll let me. I like it there. I didn't think I would at first, but now I'm getting used to it . . . besides, it's nice to be paid each week.' She frowned. 'When we—we break off our engagement, shall I have to leave?'

Oliver's face was placid, but he had dropped the lids over his dancing eyes. 'Why should you? We could—er—part in mutual friendliness. Of course you only came to Bethnal Green to get over Nicky, and if you want to return home, you're free to do so.'

Her lovely face was the picture of dismay. 'Oh—you want me to leave? I didn't know ... I thought...'

'Did I say I wanted you to leave? No such thing Celine. You're proving very useful, you can stay just as long as you want to.' He sat back while she poured their coffee, watching her. 'Shall we find somewhere to dance?' he asked.

'Dance? Us?' Her eyes flew to the clock, an ornate bronze affair on the wall. 'But it's ten o'clock; there's a clinic in the morning!'

'All the more reason for taking a little exercise now. We'll go to the Savoy. Besides, we can't start soon enough being seen together—probably there'll be someone there who knows me and who'll pass the news round.' His voice was so matter-of-fact that she could only agree. In any case, she didn't want to disagree, the prospect of dancing with him was delightful.

They danced for a couple of hours and Oliver greeted several people he knew. 'Just to set the ball rolling,' he explained, and when he drew her closer, added, 'Only in the line of duty, Celine.'

She kept her face close to his chest and willed herself to stay calm. She had thought she had been in love with Nicky, but now, loving Oliver, she discovered that this was something quite different; she was excited and happy and blissfully content all at the same time. When she had been with Nicky she had worried about her hair, her face, always taking care not to vex him, working hard at pleasing him, but with Oliver it was quite the contrary. She didn't think he'd mind if her hair looked frightful or she forgot her make-up or had a streaming cold, and since he showed no signs of ill temper, she never bothered to worry about vexing him. She said softly: 'This is nice,' and then wished that she had never said it, because he didn't reply.

He took her back about midnight, getting out of the car and opening the door and seeing her safely inside. When she thanked him for her evening he smiled slowly. 'The first of several, if we're going to do the thing properly. Goodnight, Celine.'

He held the door and she went past him, wishing with all her heart that he would kiss her. But he didn't. She heard him shut the door behind her and drive away at once.

She slept soundly, although she hadn't expected to. Too much had happened all at once, and she went down to the surgery with mixed feelings. It would be heaven to see Oliver again, but she wasn't sure if she could bear seeing him day after day, loving him so much and he not caring a button for her. He liked her, she knew that now, but liking wasn't loving, and it seemed to her that if you liked someone as a friend you weren't likely to fall in love with her. She went into the waiting-room and opened the windows, then laid out the magazines and children's books ready for the day's work.

Oliver didn't come. David Slater arrived, bringing Peter Trent with him, and since Nurse Byng was there as well as Sister Griffiths, the clinic, large though it was, was dealt with on time. The afternoon session was small, so that the three of them were able to have a leisurely lunch before opening the doors once more. And this time it was Peter Trent who arrived to see the patients. Celine contrived to ask casually if he would be there that evening too, and was horribly disappointed to hear that he would. She had somehow expected to see Oliver; he had given her the strong impression that he wanted to see her as often as possible—or so she had thought, but perhaps that was wishful thinking. She cleared up once more, readied the place for the evening clinic, then went upstairs to have her tea, a meal she ate in the solitude of her room, although she would have liked to have shared it with Mrs Thatch in her kitchen. She had poured her tea and taken a slice of bread and butter without any enthusiasm when there was a knock at the door and Oliver came in.

She put the bread and butter down. 'Oh,' she said, her breath uneven at the sight of him. 'I didn't hear you . . . I thought you weren't coming.'

He grinned at her. 'Expecting me? I'm flattered. May I share your tea?'

'Yes, of course. I'll get another cup . . .'

'Mrs Thatch is bringing it, I asked her to.' And at her look he flung up a hand. 'I know—the uninvited guest, the arrogance of the male, taking too much for granted, but I can plead hunger.'

'You've had no lunch? Why doesn't anyone see that you get something? You'd better have an egg with your tea.'

But this laudable intention was made unnecessary by the entrance of Mrs Thatch, bearing another tray, piled with sandwiches, two boiled eggs, a quantity of buttered toast and another pot of tea. 'There, sir,' she said in a motherly voice, 'you just eat that up—such a big man too to do without his victuals, we can't have you falling ill.' She glanced at Celine. 'You just see that he finishes the lot, miss.'

'There's a sizeable clinic this evening, isn't there?' asked Oliver.

'Yes—but Peter Trent's here as well as you.'

He took this gratuitous bit of information with a nod and fished a paper out of his pocket. 'See if that's all right, will you? I'll phone it through first thing in the morning.'

Celine read what he had written and then read it again. 'How did you know that my second name was Petronella?' and then: 'Do you have to send this? I mean, since we're only pretending . . .'

'Ah, but think carefully, we know we're pretending, but no one else does.'

She glanced up at him. 'You didn't tell me how you know about Petronella.'

He raised his brows. 'I asked your mother.'

'You mean she knows—and Father too?'

'Yes. But I told them you'd be ringing them up this evening and explaining.'

'Did they mind?'

'Apparently not. In fact your mother seemed to think it was a very sensible thing to do, since Nicky was proving himself to be a nuisance.'

'They weren't surprised?'

'Er—oh, yes, of course.' Oliver had eaten half the sandwiches at a great rate and Celine wondered if he'd missed his breakfast too. There was, after all, an awful lot of him to nourish. She glanced at her watch. The clinic was due to open in fifteen minutes; she would have to go down.

'You want to go? I'll drive you back to my place after we close. There are things we have to talk about.' Oliver finished the sandwiches and started on the toast. He put out a hand. 'Shall I have that back—the details are correct?'

'Yes. Must you put Petronella? Not many people know that's one of my names.'

'Then it's time they did. When I have a daughter that shall be her name—I like it.'

'Your wife might not like it,' said Celine tartly.

His eyes twinkled. 'Then I shall have to think of a way of getting round her, shan't I?'

The idea saddened her so much that she jumped to her feet. 'I'd better go—please stay here and finish your tea.'

He got up and opened the door for her, carrying her tea tray to save Mrs Thatch's feet. 'I'll be down presently,' he told her. 'I must do this more often—I seem to have been missing out on domestic comforts!'

She paused to look at him. 'Good heavens, you have all the comfort you could possibly want in your house!'

He looked annoyingly meek and apologetic. 'But not you,' he said.

Celine hurried down to the clinic and opened the doors, and was soon busy sorting out the patients while her thoughts raced. Oliver need not think he could bamboozle her in that fashion. They were agreed that their engagement was to be for one purpose only, to get rid of Nicky's attentions; it was a kind of business arrangement between friends. That she wished with her whole heart that it was nothing of the kind was beside the point. She concentrated fiercely on the delight of spending the evening with him, and when he went along to his office presently, she was as coolly efficient as she knew how to be.

The evening went slowly as sometimes it did, with tiresome patients and weary mothers and

Sister Griffiths with an evening off, but it finally came to an end and Celine began her round of clearing up jobs, only to find when she had finished them that Oliver was still deep in paper work.

'Half an hour,' he called as she whisked past the open door, 'and I'll have to call in at my rooms on the way.'

She showered and did her face and hair, then brooded over her wardrobe. The alternative to the Italian knitted was the yellow crêpe. It would have to do, because there was nothing else. She put it on, thrust her feet into high-heeled sandals, saw that she had almost ten minutes to spare and sat down on the edge of the bed, watching the clock. On no account must Oliver think her over-eager.

At one minute after the half hour she went downstairs and found him locking up. He paused to look at her. 'Nice,' he observed, and opened the surgery door, and as he settled into the car beside her: 'Shan't be long now.'

His consulting-rooms were in Wimpole Street, something Celine hadn't known. She stayed in the car while he went in and wondered what else there was to talk about. The announcement of their engagement would be in the paper in a day's time; her parents had been told, there didn't seem to be anything else. She supposed they would go out from time to time to make it all look genuine, and later, perhaps when she had gone home, it would be quietly finished. Because, of course, she would have to leave Bethanal Green. To see Oliver, if not every day, then most days, would be rather more than she would be able to bear. Besides, she might give herself away. She went hot at the very idea, and as a consequence when he got back into the car she was cool to the point of coldness, so that he presently asked her what had happened to annoy her. Celine made haste to say that it was nothing, and he didn't pursue the subject but began to talk about little Linda, doing nicely in hospital. 'You did very well there,' he told her. 'We shall miss you when you leave.'

And yet not so long ago he had assured her that there would be no need for her to leave. She said: 'Well, I suppose I shall have to go home eventually.'

They were almost there. 'Well, I hardly imagine you'll spend the rest of your life at the surgery. And when you've quite forgotten Nicky, you'll fall in love again, and this time it will be the right man.'

'Oh, but I have forgotten him.' It was on the tip of her tongue to tell him that she had fallen in love again, just as he had said, only he might ask her who it was.

Oliver must have found time to phone from his office, for Pym admitted them before he could get his door key out and showed no surprise at seeing Celine, indeed he greeted her in the same fatherly manner as Barney did at home. He took the thin shawl she had brought with her, led the way to the drawing-room and departed to tell Mrs Pym to serve dinner at once.

But there was time for a drink first and a boisterous welcome from the two small dogs. Oliver, in a great winged chair by an open window, his long legs stretched out before him, spoke thoughtfully.

'That's a pretty dress—but you always look

nice, Celine. How pleasant it is to sit here—a dress rehearsal of a kind.' And at her look of questioning surprise: 'In ten years' time, safely married, we shall remember this.'

Celine knew she would never forget it, but she felt a flicker of sympathy for his wife. It was hardly fair on her if he were to sit daydreaming about someone else. 'No, you won't,' she said matter-of-factly, 'because you'll have your wife there.'

His eyes gleamed beneath their lids. 'So I shall,' he agreed placidly, and since Pym came at that moment to tell them that dinner was served, no more was said.

It was later, as they sat over coffee in the drawing-room, that Celine reminded him that he had wanted to discuss something.

'Ah, yes! I think we should visit my aunt and uncle, don't you?' Without giving her the chance to reply: 'Next Sunday for lunch, I suggest.'

'He—Nicky won't be there?'

'Unlikely, but all the better if he is, don't you agree? And the weekend following I think I can get away for Saturday and Sunday; we could go home—your home.'

She looked down at the two dogs, sitting beside her and bent to tickle their heads. 'If you think that's a good idea. And you can spare the time. I haven't telephoned home yet.' She glanced up at him. 'I haven't had time.'

For answer he got up and dialled a number on the telephone near his chair. In a moment he handed it to her. 'Go ahead.'

It was really very difficult talking to her mother while he sat there, unashamedly listening. Her mother knew, of course, but that didn't prevent her asking awkward questions, like did Celine love Oliver and did he love her and when were they going to get married. Celine, her colour high, answered guardedly and didn't look at Oliver, which was just as well, because his smile would have infuriated her. As soon as she could, she interrupted her parent ruthlessly, told her that they would be coming for the weekend very shortly, and hung up. Oliver had told her that he had explained to her parents, but obviously her mother had got it all wrong; she would have to have it all explained to her again properly this time.

She said coldly: 'Mother seems to think—that is, perhaps you didn't explain the—the situation clearly to her.'

His voice was placid. 'Suppose you explain clearly to me—what does your mother think?'

She said tartly, 'Why, that we're properly engaged—I mean, that we're going to get married. She hasn't realised that it's just a convenience.'

'No? Ah, well, we'll put her right when we go down. Just as well, perhaps, because if Nicky should phone your home she won't have to do a lot of fibbing.'

Celine reluctantly agreed. 'But I'll have to explain,' she insisted.

'Of course you must.' Oliver was at his most genial, 'but don't try and explain to aunt and uncle, will you? Aunt Mary is a darling, and if she knew the truth and Nicky suspected it, he'd have wheedled it out of her in no time.' He got up and crossed over to the sofa to where she was sitting, put his coffee cup on the tray before her, and sat down beside her. 'I have to go to Holland in a couple of weeks—a seminar at Leiden for two days. I should like you to come with me.'

Her heart set up a tattoo of delight, although she protested at once: 'But how can I? I work at the surgery . . .'

'So do I,' he reminded her dryly. 'I daresay they'll manage for a day or two without us. And you'll be working—someone will have to see that I get there on time and eat and keep appointments. Do you speak French?'

Celine nodded, speechless.

'Good, it'll probably come in handy.'

'Don't they speak Dutch in Holland?' she managed inanely.

'Naturally, but there'll be a lot of us from all over the place, and French is widely spoken.'

'Don't you speak it?' she wanted to know.

'The odd word.' He added decisively: 'Good, that's settled. Have you a passport?'

She shook her head, found her voice and said: 'I haven't agreed to go yet . . .'

'But, my dear girl, imagine the gossip it would give rise to—just engaged, and you staying behind while I go junketing off to the Continent!' He sounded very convincing, so she said:

'Oh, well, then I'll come. My passport's out of date.'

'We'll see to it tomorrow.' He smiled at her and she melted inside, and then pulled herself together with a jerk. 'I must go back, please, it's quite late.'

He disappointingly agreed at once and drove her back, talking about nothing much as they went, the little dogs sitting side by side on the back seat. Celine wished them goodnight as she got out of the car, then she waited beside Oliver while he took her key from her and opened the door.

'Thank you for my dinner,' she said politely, and was taken utterly by surprise when he swept her into his arms and kissed her.

He didn't hurry about it, when he finally let her go he said mildly:

'I fancy we're both a little out of practice—a few rehearsals won't come amiss. Be sure to remind me.'

Celine had been kissed more times than she could count, but never once had she had to remind anyone to do so. Her charming bosom heaved with annoyance. 'I shall do no such thing!' she snapped, and sailed through the doorway, taking no notice of his quiet, 'Goodnight,' and racing up the stairs as though her life depended on it.

It was a good thing she couldn't see the look of amusement on Oliver's face as he got back into the car. The very pronounced gleam in his eyes might have disturbed her too; as it was she went to bed in a fine temper. She wasn't at all sure why she was so angry; she loved him, of course, nothing was going to alter that, but he infuriated her at times. In bed, though, she came to the tearful conclusion that she wasn't angry at all, only very unhappy.

She was more cheerful in the morning. She had got herself into an awkward situation, but she could see no way out of it—if she drew back now, Oliver would want to know why, and what was she to tell him? Better to go on as she had started, and in a few weeks, when Nicky had finally learnt to leave her alone, she would give up her job and go home. Oliver, she felt sure, wouldn't miss her. She blinked away tears at that; there was no point in making herself unhappy by thinking of a future without him.

She went down to the clinic and bustled around and kept herself busy all day. It should have helped to discover that Oliver wasn't coming in, but it didn't.

He was there on the following day, though, to receive the astonished congratulations of his staff with calm politeness. Celine had forgotten all about the announcement to be made in *The Times* and the *Telegraph*, and was almost as surprised as they were, though she managed to hide it under an exterior almost as calm as Oliver's.

It was at lunchtime, shared with Maggie Griffiths and Dorothy Byng, when she found herself bombarded with questions. When were they going to marry? Where would they live? What would she wear for the wedding? What was her ring like?

She answered them all to the best of her ability and wondered if Oliver had forgotten about a ring. There would surely be one lying around somewhere in his lovely house—some valueless trinket inherited from aunts or grandmothers or even his mother, anything would do . . .!

It seemed it wouldn't. That evening, after the clinic had finished and she had tidied up, and since there was no sign of Oliver, she was on the point of going upstairs, when he opened his office door and invited her in.

'I hadn't forgotten,' he told her, 'but I keep my mother's jewellery at the bank.'

The box he handed her was small, red leather and old. Celine opened it slowly and let out a small sigh of delight at the ring inside. Sapphires and diamonds, large ones, set in gold, worn thin with age.

'It's handed down,' explained Oliver. 'The wives have it in turn, on loan, so to speak.'

'It's beautiful!' breathed Celine. 'But I couldn't possibly wear it.'

'Why not?'

'It wouldn't be right—I mean, we're not truly engaged, you see.'

Oliver said slowly: 'I don't for one moment doubt that either my mother or any one of the Seymour wives would object—it's in a good cause, you see. Put it on.'

It fitted very well. She had large, beautifully shaped hands, well kept, the nails oval and delicately pink; the ring was exactly right.

'Suppose I should lose it?'

'I thought of that.' He dug an enormous hand into a pocket and pulled out a fine gold chain. 'You can wear it round your neck during working hours.' He glanced at the clock. 'I'm sorry, Celine, but I have to go out this evening. Will you be all right?'

Her head was instantly full of speculation. Dining with some lovely girl? Perhaps the girl who would wear his ring one day, knowing that she was entitled to do so? She said coolly: 'Of course. I don't expect you to take me out every night, you know, only when it's necessary.'

She was disconcerted when he agreed pleasantly. It would serve him right if Nicky arrived one evening and persuaded her to go out with him. She had no intention of doing so, of course, but it pleased her to imagine Oliver's reaction when she told him. She bade him a cold goodnight and bounced upstairs, where she ate a solitary supper without appetite, washed her hair, did her nails and finally went to bed early.

CHAPTER EIGHT

CELINE saw very little of Oliver until the Sunday morning. There had been little opportunity to say anything to each other until then, only as he had left on the Friday evening he had told her to be ready by ten o'clock on the Sunday, casting this over one shoulder as he hurried through the door. 'And don't forget about your passport,' he had added.

Maggie Griffiths watched him go with a sympathetic glance at Celine. 'They've admitted two children with suspected polio; he's going to see them now—they phoned not five minutes ago. Being married to a doctor isn't all roses, you'll see—working for him is bad enough!' She smiled suddenly. 'But I wouldn't mind telling you that if I were as young and pretty as you are, I'd do my best to cut you out!'

So Celine spent her Saturday walking in the park, phoning her mother and rearranging her hair in a variety of ways with a view to looking her best on the morrow.

Half way through the afternoon Mrs Thatch came to tell her she was wanted on the phone, and she raced downstairs. It would be Oliver; perhaps he was going to take her out after all. She picked up the phone and said 'Yes?' and so much of her pleasure and delight was in that one small word that Nicky exclaimed: 'You're glad to hear from me!—admit it, Celine. And don't think I believe a word about this engagement of yours—of all the nonsense—has Oliver cast a spell over you? You can't possibly love him!'

Celine said quietly: 'I don't want to talk to you, Nicky. Oliver and I are engaged and I'm very happy. Goodbye.' She rang off and went and told Mrs Thatch not to answer the phone if it should ring again during the next hour or so. It would have been lovely if she could have talked to Oliver, but nothing would have induced her to have intruded into his private life. All the same, she would tell him about it when she saw him in the morning.

The phone rang again almost immediately, and then again half an hour later, and again a third time, and by now Mrs Thatch was out with Mr Thatch doing her Saturday afternoon shopping. Celine switched on the TV in Mrs Thatch's sitting-room and doggedly watched a tennis match without seeing a thing. Presently she got up and went along to the kitchen to make a cup of tea. She had filled the kettle and was about to put it on the stove when she heard the street door being opened. Mrs Thatch hadn't been gone more than an hour, and since she and her husband always had a cup of tea out she didn't get back until well after six o'clock. Celine turned off the gas and went to peer over the banisters.

Oliver was in the hall. He said testily: 'Why in hell's name don't you answer the phone when it rings?' His stare became a frown. 'You're as white as a sheet—what's wrong?'

She peered at him from the top of the stairs. She had been scared, blissfully relieved to see him and now furious because he had snapped at her so impatiently. She said with great dignity which sat ill on her pale face: 'I didn't answer the phone because Nicky keeps ringing, and when you came in I was afraid he'd found a key . . .'

He came up the stairs two at a time and wrapped her close in a comforting embrace. 'Oh, my poor girl—what an unthinking brute I am! Come and sit down and I'll make a cup of tea and then take you back to my place.'

It was a tempting offer, but she resisted it. 'That's very kind of you, but there's no need. So silly of me to be scared, but I'm perfectly all right now.' It would be lovely to stay in his arms for ever, she thought dreamily, but that just wouldn't do.

'Mrs Pym will be disappointed; I asked her to have tea ready for us both in half an hour.'

'You want me to come to tea with you? I thought—that is, we're spending Sunday together . . .' She had been looking at him, now she turned her head away from his amused smile.

'We've still got a few things to talk over,' Oliver pointed out.

'Oh, is that why you telephoned?'

Celine had moved a little way away from him, and he put his hands in his pockets and leaned against the stair rail. He said evenly, 'I telephoned because I wanted to see you.' He didn't tell her that after the second no reply he had got into the car and driven across London just to check that she was all right. 'Shall I make that cup of tea, or shall we go now?'

She had the colour back in her cheeks again, she said a little breathlessly: 'We'll go now, if you like—I'll get my handbag.' She looked down at herself; she was wearing a plain linen dress, beautifully cut. 'Will I do like this?'

His glance was unflatteringly brief. 'Of course.'

It had been silly of her to ask, she thought, scribbling a note for Mrs Thatch. She must remember not to do that again; he was getting her out of an awkward hole, but that didn't mean he had to be personal about it.

All the same, she was happy sitting beside him as he drove to his house. By the time she got back to Bethnal Green the Thatches would be home too and she would get them to answer the phone; and tomorrow wasn't too far off now. It was a lovely afternoon, the sun sparkled on the river and the house, as Oliver pulled up in front of it, looked enchanting.

They had their tea in the garden and Celine, lulled into somnolence by Mrs Pym's delicious scones and several cups of Earl Grey, together with Oliver's gentle undemanding conversation, closed her eyes and went to sleep, her lovely head lolling back on the padded cushions of the garden chair, her mouth very slightly open.

Oliver sat opposite her, watching, and when Pym came out to collect the tea things, waved him away. It was almost an hour later when she woke up and exclaimed unnecessarily: 'I've been to sleep—I'm so sorry, how rude!'

Oliver smiled. 'I had a lot to think about,' he told her. 'It's very peaceful here and it's nice just to be able to idle for a while.'

Celine sat up and poked at her hair with her hands, and he said: 'You look perfectly all right, you can tidy up presently. Some friends asked us along for a drink later—they live a few doors away and I think you'll like them.'

She blinked at him. 'Yes, but ... aren't I going back to Bethnal Green? It's long after five o'clock.' She added worriedly: 'I'm not dressed ...'

'Why do women fuss so much about their clothes?' he asked placidly. 'You look perfectly all right. Will you come?' He paused. 'Unless you had anything else to do this evening?'

She said quietly: 'No, nothing, and I'd like to come with you.' After a moment she added: 'You're not just being kind, are you?'

'No, Celine, I'd like you to come and afterwards we can come back here for dinner—you haven't seen the house yet, have you?' He went on smoothly: 'It would be as well if you were familiar with it, don't you think? And for the record, I'm rising thirty-six, I was christened Oliver Edmund Frederick, born in a small village called Pepperham in Buckinghamshire, no brothers or sisters, parents dead. That'll do to go on with, I think, although no one is likely to cross-examine you.' He got up and pulled her to her feet. 'Mrs Pym will take you upstairs.'

His friends lived a few hundred yards away, in a house similar to his own but a good deal untidier. Eileen and Jim Weatherby had three children at home, the eldest fifteen, a schoolboy with a freckled face and an engaging grin, and two girls, one twelve, the other seven. Celine found herself accepted at once; Eileen said happily: 'Oh, here you are at last, and every bit as pretty as Oliver said you were—prettier, but you know what men are when they're in love, poor besotted creatures. I'm not surprised that he's besotted with you, love.' She smiled at Oliver and called over her shoulder: 'Come over here, Jim, and meet this lovely creature Oliver's snatched for himself!'

Celine had gone pink. Nothing, but nothing, would make her look at Oliver: all the same she was conscious of strong disappointment when he was led away to speak to someone or other at the end of the room. He was back before she could feel lost, taking her arm and introducing her to a dozen people who all seemed glad to meet her, wishing her well, asking her when they were to be married and did she like Oliver's house and would she mind being a doctor's wife. She made all the right answers, and if her colour was heightened those who saw it approved; a nice shy girl, just right for Oliver, they told each other. She was made to show her ring a dozen times too, making smiling rejoinders to everyone's remarks about it, conscious of a bitter sorrow that before long she would take it off her finger and give it back to Oliver—probably all these nice people would think her fickle and say it was a good thing that he found out that he'd made a mistake before they were married.

The party lasted some time, and they were among the first to leave, Oliver giving the excuse that he had to telephone the hospital about one of his patients. As they strolled the short distance back to his house he observed: 'There aren't many advantages to being a doctor, but it's so convenient to be called away for urgent phone messages.'

'No patient needing your attention?'

'Not that I know of. Peter is on call, anyway.'

'But do you go on call too?' She added apologetically: 'I don't know much about your work.'

'Well, no, I don't. But I can be contacted if someone wants advice.'

'Oh, are you a consultant?'

'Yes.' They had reached the house and went inside. 'Do you want another drink before dinner?' asked Oliver.

She shook her head. 'No, thanks. Will you tell me about your work?'

They were in the sitting-room, looking out of the window at the river. 'Nothing much to tell. I specialise in children's diseases; I've got consulting rooms—you've been to them; I run the clinic and I have beds in several hospitals. Occasionally I travel if I'm wanted somewhere.'

'Abroad as well as here?'

'Yes.'

'Oh, are you important?'

He smiled. 'Let's say that if I dropped down dead tomorrow there would be someone else to fill my shoes.'

'Don't,' she spoke vehemently, 'talk like that! I think you're important.'

'I'm flattered. Ah, here's Pym—I'm famished!'

Over dinner he told her something of the forthcoming trip to Holland.

'The end of next week,' he told her. 'We shall be gone for four days. I'll take the car and we'll go from Harwich on the night ferry. We shall be staying with some friends of mine in Leiden—Dr

Theo ter Boen; he has a French wife, Mireille. There are a clutch of children too, I'm not sure how many, four at the last count, I believe.'

'I've got no clothes,' said Celine suddenly.

'Not enough for four days? My dear girl, it's not a social visit—all you'll need is a dress for the days, and something different for the evenings. That yellow thing would do very nicely.'

Celine eyed him a trifle crossly. 'I've had it for years!'

'What a splendid wife you'll make. No one will know that, you can take that other thing you wear—Italian, isn't it?' She looked at him in surprise and he said mildly: 'I'm quite observant, it must be something to do with being a doctor.'

She laughed. 'Don't be so silly! Only I don't want to let you down by looking dowdy.'

'You could never look that, Celine. Got your passport?'

'Yes. One of those visitors' passports from the Post Office.'

'Good. Apply for a normal one, will you? You never know when you might want to travel in the future.'

'It's very unlikely.' She looked at him in surprise. 'When I get home it'll be Mother and Father who'll need a holiday; I suppose the bed and breakfast trade will die out at the end of the summer and I can manage very well on my own. They'll need a rest.'

Oliver asked idly: 'They're making a go of it, are they?'

'Yes, much more so than we ever imagined.'

They sat over their coffee in the sitting-room, watching the evening pale and then darken gradually. It was eleven o'clock by the time Oliver sent the Aston Martin sliding back towards Bethnal Green. The street was quiet and the surgery looked bleak indeed after Oliver's house. Celine, standing beside him while he unlocked the door, wished with all her heart that she was back there. Oliver handed her back the key, held the door open for her and glanced over his shoulder into the hall. There was no letter there—she had looked too.

'Glanced at that star of yours lately?' asked Oliver.

She looked up. 'No—but I know it's still there.' She lowered her eyes and met his.

'Oh, good,' said Oliver, and kissed her hard. 'I did say that we needed to practise,' he reminded her, and pushed her gently indoors. Celine stood in the narrow little hall listening to the subdued roar of the car gradually receding. A clock somewhere or other struck midnight and she smiled. It was Sunday today—this very morning she would be seeing Oliver again.

The Seymours lived in a handsome house set in a large garden on the outskirts of Highgate; twice as large as Oliver's, but, thought Celine privately, not half as nice. It was elaborately late Victorian, with old-fashioned sash windows and a large conservatory running the width of the house at the back, where Mr Seymour pottered among his plants. He was getting around now, although he would never be quite the same again, for he had a slight limp and one arm was still weak. All the same, he greeted Celine with pleasure, assured her that he had never felt better in his life before and bore her off to admire his Browallia. 'Your father has some in your greenhouse, but I venture to think that mine are better specimens.'

Celine admired colour, size and height and spent the next half hour touring the array of plants and flowers. Oliver, she was quick to notice, had settled himself comfortably in a garden chair beside his aunt and was deep in conversation. She admired an arum lily with insincerity and longed for a cool drink.

Someone must have read her thoughts, because a moment later an elderly woman came out with a tray loaded with glasses and jugs and bottles and Mrs Seymour bade them come and sit down.

Over iced lemonade, Celine answered questions, and there were a great many of them, and all the while Oliver sat there, saying almost nothing, indeed looking to be on the verge of taking a nap. He made no sign when a car's engine sounded faintly from the front of the house, and although he got up as the door opened, his face wore its usual placid expression. Celine, turning to look too, sat rigid in her chair. Nicky had walked in and his wife with him.

Celine shot one fulminating look at Oliver, who returned it with a calm stare, and pinned a smile to her flushed face as she greeted Daphne and nodded with what she hoped was friendly nonchalance to Nicky. It helped a lot to see that he had been taken by surprise too, and showed it. Indeed, once she had got over the initial shock, she found she wasn't minding meeting him again in the least; he just didn't matter any more. They sat and talked for a while before going in to lunch—a lengthy elaborate meal in a vast, heavily furnished dining-room and when they went back to the conservatory for their coffee, Daphne suggested to Celine that they might walk round the garden. 'Mother-in-law has a nap,' she confided, 'and the men like a talk—usually I'm on my own for an hour, and I never know what to do.'

'You come every Sunday?' asked Celine.

'Mostly. We didn't for a while—when we decided to get a divorce, you know, but we're having another go yet again, because of Mandy.'

She took Celine's arm as they started to stroll across the wide lawn.

'I don't suppose it will work, though. Nicky just has to have girl-friends—they don't mean anything, I suppose, but it's humiliating.' She turned her head to smile at Celine. 'How are you enjoying working for Oliver? He is a pet, isn't he? Have you been to his house? You must have done—silly of me to ask now you're engaged.'

'Yes, I like it very much—we had drinks with some friends of his, the Weatherbys, and I met quite a few people.'

'He's very well liked. I can't think why he hasn't been snapped up long before this. Not,' Daphne added hastily, 'that you ... that is, I'm sure the boot was on the other foot; you're so pretty you could pick and choose ... Oliver had some sort of an affair years and years ago; Nicky always swore it put him off women for ever and ever, but he was just biding his time, waiting for you. I'm sure you'll be happy. When are you going to get married?'

Celine was beginning to wish that she hadn't come. Daphne was a dear, but getting rather too inquisitive. 'We haven't decided,' she said pleasantly. 'We've only been engaged a little while, and Oliver's a busy man.'

'I don't suppose you see much of him?'

'Well, most days he comes to the surgery, but of course I'm a kind of general help there and there's very little time to talk,' Celine explained.

'Oh, well, you'll see plenty of him once you're married. We'd better go back, I suppose, Nicky wants to call in on some friends on the way home and I'd like to be back to say goodnight to Mandy.'

As they neared the house, Daphne said suddenly with a little laugh: 'It's lucky you're engaged to Oliver; you're exactly the kind of girl Nicky goes for!' She bent to smell a rose and Celine had time to compose her face into polite interest.

'Oh, really?' she asked, and then, because she had pinkened a little, 'Isn't it hot? It will be quite nice to sit in the shade for a while. Do you suppose the men will have finished their talk?'

'I should think so. Nicky can't stand Oliver, you know, because Oliver's successful and he's not. He's got an allowance and plays around in Father-in-law's firm, but he's bone idle and selfish. Do you think I'm awful talking like this?' Daphne added, 'I'm disloyal, aren't I?' Her voice was bitter. 'But he's been disloyal to me times without number.'

'I think you're a very good wife,' said Celine. 'If it had been me I should have given up a long time ago. But I expect you love him.'

'That's what Oliver always says.'

Nicky and Daphne left presently, and Celine, with Oliver's hand tucked under her arm, wished them goodbye with just the right amount of friendly warmth. There had been one bad moment when Nicky had contrived to get her alone for a few seconds. 'Am I supposed to believe that this is a fairytale romance?' he sneered in a whisper. 'Anyone less romantic than Oliver I've yet to meet.' He added savagely: 'You'll be telling me next that you love him.'

Celine looked into his angry face. 'Yes, I do, Nicky.' She spoke quietly and with conviction, and he drew back, nonplussed. A moment later Oliver had taken her arm; she could feel his large firm hand, very reassuring, clasping her elbow. She relaxed at once and then drew a startled breath; perhaps he had heard what she had said ... But apparently he hadn't, for his manner hadn't changed; he was calmly good natured, just as usual.

They went out to dinner that evening after a lazy tea at his house, with dogs tumbling round them while Oliver went into details about their trip. Celine listened with only half an ear because it was so nice just to sit there and watch his face and listen to his voice.

'I doubt if you've heard a word,' observed Oliver. 'What's on your mind, Celine?'

'Nothing—nothing, really.' Her denial was so emphatic that he gave her a searching glance. But he didn't repeat his question, merely suggested that if they were going out she might like to go upstairs and tidy herself.

He took her to the Savoy Grill Room, and over lobster and salad and strawberries and cream, helped down by champagne, questioned her gently about her home. He did it so well that she was quite unaware of the amount of information she had given him.

Later, as he opened the surgery door for her, she hoped he would kiss her again, but he didn't, only made a casual remark about the busy day ahead of them tomorrow, and when she thanked him for her day, murmured politely.

Beyond saying hullo to each other, they didn't speak more than half a dozen words on Monday. Tuesday wasn't much better, and on Wednesday Oliver didn't come until after the morning clinic was over. But then things began to look up. Oliver stopped on his way to his office.

'Doing anything this evening?' he wanted to know. 'The Weatherbys have asked us in for a drink. We could have dinner afterwards—it'll have to be at home because I'm expecting one or two calls from the hospital.'

Celine changed happily after she had cleared the clinic and made sure that everything was ready for the next day. She had decided on the apricot silk, and surveying herself in the long mirror in the bathroom, she wondered if she would take it to Holland. Would Oliver take her out, she wondered, or would he be busy every minute of each day there? She decided to play safe and take it with her.

She was feeling so happy that it came as a shock when Oliver observed quietly as they drove through London: 'You're cured of Nicky, aren't you, Celine?' And when she nodded without speaking: 'All the same, I hope you'll stay with us for a while, and I suggest we stay engaged for the little bit longer just to throw Nicky off the scent. If either of us wants to tell anyone special about the true state of affairs, there's no reason why we shouldn't, as long as it's for their ears alone.'

Celine was puzzled at that, but there wasn't really time to think about it, because they had arrived at the house, and a few minutes later, leaving it outside his own front door, they were at the Weatherbys.

There weren't as many people there this time, although Celine recognised several faces from the previous party. She was handed from one group to the next, a glass in her hand, exchanging lighthearted talk, wishing Oliver was beside her and not at the other end of the room. Mrs Weatherby prised her away presently, though. 'I've been dying to talk to you, and now we'll have five minutes gossip. Come and sit over here. Since we're to be neighbours we really must get to know each other. Oliver tells me you live in Dorset in a lovely old manor house; you must find London very different, although we all love it here.'

'Well, so do I,' said Celine happily. 'I think Oliver's house is super—of course, it's not very nice in Bethnal Green, but I do like working there.'

'But you'll not work once you're married? I'm sure Oliver wouldn't want you to do that. You don't know how delighted we are to see him settled at last. I was beginning to think he really was waiting for Hilary . . .'

'Hilary?' asked Celine, her happiness suddenly uncertain.

'Our daughter—bless the girl, she always declared she would marry Oliver, you know, and he . . . well, you know how it is, he used to laugh and say she was a bit young for him—they've known each other for years, of course, and he's very fond of her.' Mrs Weatherby laughed, a nice jolly laugh, quite devoid of malice. 'I daresay if he hadn't found you he might have waited. You must meet her when she comes home.'

'Yes, I'd like to.' Celine heard her voice, quite normal, to her own surprise. So that was what he'd meant by telling the true state of affairs to someone special. This Hilary—and Celine already hated the girl with a fierce hatred she didn't know she could be capable of—was waiting quietly somewhere in the wings, not minding that Oliver was engaged because he would have explained that it was all a sham anyway and wouldn't last much longer. Celine, her fine eyes sparkling, entered into an animated discussion of the new season's clothes and presently became absorbed into yet another group.

She wasn't going to say anything to Oliver, she decided as they walked back to his house. Just as soon as she decently could, she would go back home and never, never allow him the faintest inkling of her feelings. She would have to go to Holland, of course—indeed, she would have to behave as though she had never heard of Hilary. Oliver had been kind and helped her when she had needed help so badly, but it had gone no further than that for him, and if she had been fool enough to fall in love with him, that was entirely her own silly business.

She had done well, she considered later that night as she got ready for bed. They had dined together in perfect friendliness, and afterwards Oliver had taken her on a tour of the house, a very thorough one, showing her his study and the cosy little library and the dear little sitting-room tucked behind the imposing drawing room, and then upstairs to peer into the bedrooms, all delightfully furnished, and higher still, up a corkscrew staircase to the attics, just as beautifully furnished and with their own bathrooms. The house was bigger than it appeared to be, and Celine remarked on that fact. 'All these rooms and no one in them,' she commented.

'Ah, but once the children start growing, they'll be needed,' Oliver assured her, and she hadn't been sure if he was joking or not. It hurt her to think of his children and Hilary sharing his home. 'So just stop thinking about it, you stupid girl,' she told herself sharply.

Which did no good at all, of course. She still stayed awake for most of the night, and if she was a little pale the next morning, Sister Griffiths put it down to a late night and probably, she added severely, a little too much to drink. Celine agreed meekly.

David Slater and Peter took the morning clinic, but halfway through the afternoon, Oliver arrived and David went, leaving the two of them to work their way through a fairly small number of patients. But the evening was busy again and it wasn't until they were clearing up that Oliver had time for a word with Celine. 'We'll leave tomorrow evening,' he told her. 'David will be here so that we can get away around seven o'clock. You'll be ready?'

She assured him that she would. Indeed, she had her case packed and only her night bag to fill with the last-minute odds and ends.

They left punctually, and Celine felt guilty leaving Maggie Griffiths and Dorothy behind, although neither of them seemed to mind about that. It seemed natural enough to them that since she was going to marry their chief, she should go with him whenever possible. They told her to have a good time and waved from the door as Oliver drove away.

They had plenty of time, and Oliver drove fast. At Wivenhoe he stopped at the Smugglers and they had dinner at leisure before going on to Harwich. Celine, waiting in the long queue of cars to go on board, was glad of that. It was a warm, dim evening with a hint of thunder and the delay seemed unnecessarily long, but Oliver showed no sign of impatience, keeping up a desultory flow of small talk until at last, the car safely in the ship's garage, they were on deck. Most of the passengers had gone straight to the bar or the dining-rooms, so they had room to stroll around until presently, when the ship sailed, he suggested that they have a drink and that Celine should go to her cabin. Celine would have been happy enough to have stayed up all night with him, but since the thought hadn't crossed his mind, she agreed cheerfully, accepted her drink and went briskly to bed, smothering the nasty feeling that he had actually been pleased to see her go.

She consoled herself with the thought that probably he had work to get ready for the seminar on Monday; he wouldn't have much time to prepare for that as he had told her that he had two consultations on the afternoon of their arrival and a visit to one of the hospitals on Sunday morning.

Before she fell asleep she wondered vaguely why he had wanted her to go with him; certainly she wasn't going to contribute much work. Perhaps it was for the look of the thing? They were, after all, engaged.

She slept dreamlessly and woke to the bustling activity of the Hook of Holland and the advice, brought with her morning tea and toast, that they would be disembarking in half an hour. She was just ready when there was a tap on the door and Oliver put his head round it.

'Oh, good—you're ready. We can go down to the car.' He took her overnight bag and led the way. 'Did you sleep well?'

Just for the moment, with him close by, the sunshine and all the excitement of arrival, she was happy. 'Like a top,' she declared.

Customs were brief, they were on the road north to Leiden within half an hour or so, a road streaming with fast traffic and little to see.

'Disappointed?' asked Oliver. 'This is a motor-way, missing all the villages and small towns. We leave it presently. My friends live outside Leiden in a charming house well tucked away. I think you'll like it.'

He turned off within minutes and took a narrow land road through flat country. 'Very Dutch,' observed Celine, eyeing the black and white cows, the green water-meadows and clumps of small trees, sliding into a distance which looked nearer than it was because of the flatness. 'At least,' she amended, 'it's exactly how I pictured Holland.'

'A pity we shan't have more time to drive round.' Oliver was going slowly now, the road running beside a narrow lake, swarming with boats. 'Weekend sailing,' he explained, 'a popular sport here.'

The road left the lake presently, only to join

another stretch of water on the other side. Here Oliver took a lane leading to a cluster of houses and trees on the side of the lake. 'Hungry?' he asked. 'We're almost there.'

He drove past the houses and the oversized church towering above their red-tiled roofs, along a lane beside the still water, and turned in at an open gateway. The drive was narrow, overhung with trees and bordered by thickets on either side, and beyond a glimpse of stonework ahead of them there was nothing to see. The house came into view quite suddenly; stone-built, solid, its windows sparkling in the sun, its open front door suddenly full of people and dogs.

The man who came down the steps to meet them was tall and thin and stooped a little; he was nice-looking too, with mild eyes behind thick glasses. The woman with him was small and plump with dark hair and eyes and a delicate beaky nose. Around them swarmed four children and an assortment of dogs.

Oliver got out, opened Celine's door and turned to greet his friends. He shook Theo's hand, kissed Mireille, introduced Celine and turned his attention to the children.

Theo shook her hand gravely, welcomed her with warmth and left her with Mireille. 'You are Celine,' declared that little lady, 'of whom we hear so much. Oliver tells me you speak French, for which I am so thankful—I must speak Dutch and English for most of the time, you understand, and I long to speak my own language.'

'Well, I'm a bit rusty,' said Celine, and plunged into her best French.

Minutes later, when the two men joined them

with the children, Mireille broke off to say: 'Oliver, I love you for ever—your Celine speaks my own tongue so very well. I shall not stop talking to her all the while you are here.' She twinkled at him. 'Where did you find this so lovely girl?' She gave a little laugh. 'You will not tell, I can see. Come inside and have breakfast and then Celine and I can talk some more while you men plan your day. Children, we go indoors now, and you will not be noisy.'

Considering there were four of them between the ages of ten and five, they weren't noisy at all; they were polite but not tiresomely so, and they adored Oliver. Celine, tidying herself quickly in the charming room Mireille had taken her to, tried not to think too much about that. When she had first met him, he hadn't seemed a man to be interested in children or enjoy their company, but he so obviously did both—he would be a splendid father. She crushed the wistful thought and went downstairs to the vast kitchen at the back of the house, where they all sat down at the massive table to drink coffee and eat fresh rolls and cheese and ham and cherry jam. And when they had finished Oliver came round the table to her and took her arm for a moment.

'You'll be all right? Theo and I have some talking to do and after lunch I must go into Leiden for a couple of hours. The children will look after you, and Mireille, of course. Theo says he'll drive you all down to the lake this afternoon for an hour or so.'

'That will be nice,' said Celine, dutifully enthusiastic. 'Isn't there anything I can do for you?'

'Nothing.' His eyes searched her face.

'Tomorrow there will be time for a walk in the country.' He added deliberately: 'The children love that—so do the dogs. If you're a good girl, I might take you to visit the hospital some time on Monday.'

'How kind,' said Celine gently, 'but I'm sure I'm going to be quite happy to stay here.'

She gave him a wide sweet smile, and he grinned suddenly. 'Vixen,' he said softly, and kissed her so swiftly that she hadn't even suspected he was going to.

And in front of an audience of four children, a gently amused Mireille and Theo and an assortment of dogs!

CHAPTER NINE

THE morning passed delightfully, most of it spent stretched out on a garden chair on the lawn behind the house. Celine, drinking iced lemonade and listening to Mireille's chatter, felt envy stirring inside her although she wasn't an envious girl. There was so much that Mireille had; a loving husband, and a successful one too, four charming children, a lovely old house, and from the glimpse Celine had had, sufficient staff to run it well. She was to go over the house, Mireille had promised, but later; there was time enough before lunch. So they sat in the sun while Celine described the season's clothes in London, her home in Dorset and the work she did at the surgery, interlarded with chatter from the children and a lot of barking from the dogs.

Presently they strolled indoors and Mireille took her on a leisurely tour of the house, spending a long time in the kitchen talking to a large, very stout woman—not that much was said, but since Celine's Dutch was non-existent and Maagda the cook's English was the same, so everything had to be translated and said twice. Once out of the kitchen, though, they trooped through the house, children and dogs forming a lively tail behind them, while Celine was shown pictures of ancestors, old family silver and beautifully carved furniture housed in its various rooms. Upstairs the rooms were lighter and colourful and cleverly modernised, and on the floor above there was an enormous room for the children, equipped with almost everything a child could wish for.

'This is a good idea,' declared Mireille. 'You will find that it is necessary when you have children. Oliver's house is smaller than this one, is it not? But there are bedrooms not in use, if I remember; you will have fun together, making them ready for the children when they come.'

Celine agreed with a smile that hurt; it was like having a door opened on to a wonderful landscape she would never be allowed to wander in.

Lunch was a noisy, cheerful meal, and the moment it was over, Oliver left for Leiden. When he had driven away, Mireille, standing beside Celine in the open doorway, remarked: 'You English—so cold, no kissing, not even a hand held ... you are perhaps shy?'

'Not when we're together,' said Celine with what she hoped was suitable coyness.

They all spent a lazy afternoon by the lake.

Theo had his own boat tied up to a small jetty and they went over it before the children got into the small dinghy moored alongside and invited Celine to take a trip on the water. They pottered round happily enough before they finally came ashore and went off on their own, leaving her to stretch out on the grass beside her host and hostess. She dozed off almost at once and didn't wake until Oliver slid his length down beside her and kissed the tip of her nose. As she opened her eyes and stared up into his face, so close to hers, she thought she saw a look in his eyes that sent her heart thumping, but almost immediately he had dropped the lids and she was left uncertain, so uncertain that she told herself silently that it had been nothing but wishful thinking. Besides, Theo and Mireille were both watching; he had probably kissed her because it would have been the natural thing to do.

She summoned a smile and sat up. 'I've been asleep again; that's all I seem to do. Did you have . . .' She paused, she had been going to say a busy afternoon, but did famous consultants have those? Didn't they have appointments arranged for them so that they could make their deliberations without haste? She went on: 'A successful consultation?'

'Most successful,' he told her gravely, and she looked away because she knew that under the gravity he was laughing at her.

But he behaved beautifully for the rest of that day. They dined late by candlelight and Celine, by no means conceited, couldn't help but know that the apricot silk showed to its best advantage in the gentle light, perhaps it was the combination of them both which caused him to behave exactly as a man in love should, sitting beside her on one of the enormous sofas, an arm flung behind her shoulders, not touching her or even looking at her much, but somehow conveying the impression that she was very much his. And she could see by the twinkle in Mireille's eyes that she thought the same.

They sat around talking until quite late, and when Mireille said at length that she was going to bed and Celine got up too, she could find no fault with Oliver's goodnight kiss. Her head full of foolish dreams, she took herself off to bed determined to lie and recall every minute of the evening, instead of which she fell asleep the moment her head touched the pillow.

Both Oliver and Theo left after breakfast the next morning and Celine, who had expected him to renew his suggestion that she might like to go with him to the hospital, was quite unreasonably peevish because he didn't. True, she had refused yesterday, but didn't he know that a girl could change her mind? She borrowed a bikini from Mireille and spent the morning with the children in the swimming pool at the bottom of the large garden around the house, leaving it every now and then to lie in the sun and gossip with Mireille. But when she heard the car coming up the drive she skipped indoors and spent the next half hour showering and changing into the Italian dress, to come down presently, looking very neat and rather sedate, and join the others in the garden for drinks.

They went for a walk after lunch, along the lakeside, through the water-meadows and along the brick-built lanes on top of the sleeper dykes. 'The next dyke nearer the water is a dreamer,' explained Theo, 'and the one nearest the lake is the watcher.'

They all sat down presently, because it was a warm afternoon, and watched the multitude of yachts on the lake in the distance. It was a charming sight, and Celine, listening to the casual talk with Oliver stretched out beside her, half asleep, could have stayed there for ever. But it was just as pleasant when they got back and found tea waiting for them in the garden, and presently Theo and Mireille and the children wandered off, leaving her and Oliver sitting comfortably in garden chairs.

'A pity you didn't want to come this morning,' observed Oliver presently. 'I think you might have found it interesting.'

'If you'd asked me again I would have,' said Celine crossly.

'Oh, dear—I've been wondering why I've been kept at a distance all day.'

'Nothing of the sort,' cried Celine, and felt her cheeks grow hot. 'I've been . . . well, what do you mean, anyway?'

He got up and crossed over to her chair and pulled her out of it, quite gently. 'Not enough of this,' he said, and bent and kissed her, holding her close. He went on holding her, looking down into her face, smiling a little. 'We are engaged,' he reminded her softly.

Anyone could see them from the house. She supposed unhappily that was his reason for kissing her—not that it mattered what his friends thought; she wasn't likely to see them ever again and once they were back in England it would be a simple matter to let them know, in the course of time, that she and Oliver were not to be married after all.

Oliver felt her stiffen in his arms, and released her. He said in a cool friendly voice, 'I believe Mireille has some plan for tomorrow while we're at the Seminar—a tour of Leiden and then probably on to Amsterdam.' And when Celine didn't answer: 'Theo has asked us to stay on for another day or so, but I can't spare the time. I thought we might try for the night ferry tomorrow.'

Which meant that she would see nothing of him all day. She said: 'Yes, of course, what a good idea,' and then, chattily: 'I shall enjoy seeing something of Leiden—it's the birthplace of Rembrandt, isn't it? And didn't the Pilgrim Fathers start from there? And isn't there a rather splendid canal the—Rapenburg, it's called, isn't it? Doesn't the University lie quite close to it? And the Hospital?' She paused for breath, aware that she was babbling like a tourist who knew her guide book by heart.

She peeped at Oliver and found his face impassive, which meant very probably that he was laughing at her. She said with a touch of peevishness: 'I promised the children I'd play croquet . . .'

'Ah, yes—a soothing game when the nerves are twanging a bit.'

'My nerves don't twang!' Her voice was sharp.

'My dear girl, have I said they did?' He was at his most placid, and the desire to box his ears for him was very great, only they were out of reach.

It was a good deal cooler the next day, which was a good thing, because Mireille had planned a formidable programme for them both. The two men left the house soon after eight o'clock, and as soon as the children had been bestowed into the care of an elderly woman, who, it seemed, came daily to oversee their activities during the school holidays, she urged Celine into her little Renault car and drove into Leiden.

Considering the time they had at their disposal, Mireille worked miracles. They left the car and walked into Leiden; down one side of the Rapenburg Canal and up the other, past the University and the little lane leading to the Hortus Botanicus Gardens, and then on to the other side past the Museum of Antiquities, and from there into Breestraat, the backbone of Leiden, as it were.

But Mireille had by no means finished. They did a lightning tour of the Sint Pieterskerk, the Burcht fortifications and the Cornmarket Bridge, they even managed to have a quick cup of coffee in the Doelen, on the edge of the Rapenburg Canal. Celine was still getting her breath as she was urged back into the car and Mireille started on the short drive to Amsterdam. 'Because,' she exclaimed, 'you simply must see as much as possible. Such a shame that you can't both stay another couple of days. Oliver seemed to like the idea when I suggested it at first; I suppose something has turned up.'

'He's a very busy man,' said Celine quickly.

If Mireille had achieved miracles of sightseeing in Leiden, she did even better in Amsterdam. Celine was taken on a barge tour through the canals, a brisk view of the Dam Palace and the

Dam Square, lunch in the Bijenkorf store, so that they could have a quick look round its enticing wares, a glimpse of the Beginjnhof, a group of charming almshouses tucked away behind Kalverstraat, and an even briefer glimpse of the Rijksmuseum, but only from the outside. 'Because it's time for us to go home,' said Mireille reluctantly, 'but you have seen a little of the city anyhow.'

Celine, her eyes and head aching, agreed. 'A bit rushed,' went on Mireille, 'but next time you come Oliver can take you on a more leisurely trip. I daresay you'll be married by then.'

She glanced questioningly at Celine, who went a guilty pink and muttered that she supposed so, but Mireille, who thought the pink and mutterings were shyness, was quite satisfied.

The men got back an hour or so after their own return; there was barely time to have dinner before Oliver's laconic: 'Well, it's time to go. It's been delightful—remember it's your turn to come to us. Theo, let me know what you decide about Vienna—we might go together.'

Mireille groaned: 'Not another of your meetings? Well, if you go, Celine can come here to me and you can pick her up on the way back.'

A suggestion to which Oliver agreed with what Celine took to be well assumed enthusiasm. She said all the proper things, hugged the children, allowed to stay up to see them off, and got into the car beside Oliver.

The drive was a short one, not much more than half an hour, and they talked very little. Waiting in the queue to go on board, Oliver said: 'Do you think you could start work after lunch tomorrow?

We should be at Bethnal Green by mid-morning. The thing, is Nurse Byng is off sick—Peter rang this morning—and there's a large clinic for the afternoon.' He glanced at her. 'I shall be tied up for a couple of days, so we shan't see much of each other.'

'I expect you've a lot of work to catch up on, and of course I can be ready by lunch time— earlier than that if you like. I've only got to have a shower and change.'

'After lunch will do, and thanks. Did you like Theo and Mireille and the children?'

'Very much—the children are darlings. They're a happy family, aren't they?'

'Yes—nice to see in this day and age, isn't it? Ah, good, we're moving.'

It was already late evening by the time they were on board, and Celine could only agree when Oliver suggested that she might like to go straight to her cabin. 'I'll get someone to bring you a drink,' he told her, which took away the one excuse she had had time to think up. So she went down to her cabin, drank the tea and ate the sandwiches the stewardess brought, then went to bed, where she cried herself to sleep, although she wasn't quite sure what she was crying about.

It was a dismal morning. She had got up early and gone on deck where she found a grey sky and damp tepid air which seemed to cling to everything. They were still some way off, although the coast of England was clearly visible. She had forgotten to ask about breakfast, and was leaning against the rail wondering what to do about it, when Oliver joined her.

'You're up early, Celine. Shall we have

breakfast? We shan't dock for another hour. You slept well?'

The question was casual, but he had noticed the pinkened lids and pale face. His mouth twitched at her swift: 'Oh, marvellously, thank you.'

She was thankful for the meal; for one thing she was hungry and for another it made conversation easier. They didn't hurry over it, and there was just time to go to her cabin and get her bag before the ferry docked.

They were clear of Harwich and on the way to London within half an hour, driving through drizzle now; weather to suit her mood, thought Celine. The trip to Holland hadn't been a success. She still wasn't quite sure why she had been asked to go. Oliver must have had some good reason; he was a man to have good reasons for doing anything he did, but he didn't always bother to tell anyone else about them. She essayed small-talk as they went, but it was apparent that he wanted to think undisturbed. She fell silent, and presently closed her eyes and feigned sleep, opening them rather cleverly just as he was threading his way through the last of the streets leading to the surgery. She had had to peep once or twice, of course, but she woke up in what she considered to be a most natural way, only to hear Oliver's dry voice: 'Next time you pretend to be asleep, Celine, you'd better get your breathing right—and empty your head of thoughts. I could almost hear you thinking.'

He pulled up in front of the surgery door and turned to look at her. She said in a waspish voice: 'You didn't want to talk—I thought it would be easier if I closed my eyes, but I'll remember what you say—for next time.'

She opened her door and got out before he could reach her side of the car. 'Don't do that again,' he told her severely. 'The traffic's bad along here.' He opened the door and went back to the car. 'Go on up,' he told her, 'I'll bring your case.'

Her room looked small after the large room she had had at Mireille's house. She went back to the head of the stairs just as Oliver got there. She took her bag from him and stood awkwardly, looking at him.

'Thank you for the trip,' she said finally. 'I—I enjoyed it.'

'Good.' His voice was placid, he was smiling a little. 'They'll be glad to see you downstairs later.'

He went back downstairs and Celine stood watching his enormous back disappear from her view. The relationship hadn't changed one iota, she thought drearily. He was exactly the same as when they had first met—their engagement was a farce even if it had served its purpose. The quicker she ended it the better. She went back to her room and unpacked, showered, and put on a cotton skirt and top, ate the lunch Mrs Thatch provided for her, and went downstairs to the clinic, where Maggie greeted her with a quite heartwarming relief. 'Oh, good, you're back—I thought I heard the car; didn't see Dr Seymour, though. There's a big clinic presently—if you've had your lunch will you start getting out the notes? There's a list on the desk over there.'

Celine slipped back into the routine without effort. It was nice to be kept busy, it stopped her thinking, and by the end of the day she was too tired anyway. Of Oliver there had been no sign, but he had said that they wouldn't be seeing much of each other for a few days.

It was two days more before she was able to see him again. He arrived for the morning clinic, elegant and unruffled and pleasantly businesslike, so that beyond a good morning, Celine didn't say anything more. The clinic was a long one and he prepared to go as soon as it was finished. She was in the waiting room, straightening it ready for the afternoon, as he went past the door, and he stopped.

'How about dinner this evening?' he asked. 'I think it's time we had a talk, Celine.'

She could see nothing encouraging in his manner—unapproachably pleasant, which was perhaps just as well. 'Yes, I want to talk to you, but there's no need for dinner. I can say it all in a few minutes.'

'I'm sure you can. We'll have a meal at my house, I'll come back for you at seven o'clock.'

Celine opened her mouth to make a suitable retort to this piece of arrogance, but he had gone. She finished her tidying up, reflecting that it was really not important, it didn't matter—nothing mattered now. She would say what she had to say and go back home. The prospect choked her with unshed tears.

The evening clinic was very short, all the same she had to hurry in order to be ready by seven o'clock. She got into the apricot dress, took great care with her face and hair, put on her Gucci sandals, snatched up their matching bag, told Mrs Thatch she wouldn't be late back and went downstairs, to meet Oliver opening the street door.

It annoyed her to see that he looked quite cheerful, and his placid conversation as he drove her to his house did nothing to soothe her. She was on edge herself; she felt he should be the same.

Pym greeted her with a beaming smile and left them alone in the drawing-room, and Celine, uncertain as to how much time she had before dinner should be announced, sat uncertainly, a glass of sherry in her hand, rehearsing her opening sentence.

'I should wait until we've had a meal,' observed Oliver calmly. 'It's easier to talk on a full stomach.'

She considered this unanswerable, and it was as well that Pym chose that moment to tell them that Mrs Pym had dished up.

The meal was delicious. It seemed to Celine that Mrs Pym had cooked everything she enjoyed most, all the same she found that she had no appetite, although she did her best. Oliver on the other hand enjoyed his meal, keeping up a steady flow of talk, apparently unnoticing of her brief comments and long silences. But presently they went back to the drawing-room and Celine poured their coffee with a hand which shook very slightly, so that Oliver asked: 'Nervous, Celine? I wonder why?'

It was now or never, and surely he would be as pleased as she was to get the matter settled. Thus heartened by this quite inaccurate view of her own feelings, she put down her cup. 'Oliver——' she began, and found her nicely thought out speech had flown. But there was no stopping her now. She said in a rush: 'I've quite got over Nicky. Even if he phones or I met him, I wouldn't care any more. He's just—just nothing. So we don't have to be engaged any more. I'm most grateful to you for all you've done, I really am, and it must have been tiresome for you—I mean pretending, that we were going to be married when all the while it was ... well, never mind that.'

She was looking straight at him, hoping to see some hint of his own feelings, but his face was impassive, even faintly amused. She took the ring carefully off her finger and put it on the table beside her. 'I won't need that any more—thank you for letting me wear it. I'd like to go home as soon as possible—I mean, you'll want to get someone else, won't you, but I ... there's heaps for me to do at home ...' She faltered under his steady stare and ended lamely: 'That's all.'

When he didn't speak she said: 'I expect you're as glad to be free as I am,' and then: 'Well, do say something!'

He said at last: 'My dear Celine, what is there to say? Naturally I'm pleased to hear that you've got over Nicky. Shall I add that I hope we'll be the best of friends in the future.' His voice was suddenly harsh. 'You're quite certain that this is what you want to do, aren't you? You didn't like me much at first, did you, but I had thought you were beginning to like me.'

'Oh, I do,' said Celine feverishly, wishing this was all over and done with and she was back in her room enjoying a good weep. She went on talking at random. 'It's so nice to have friends, isn't it? You've a great number, haven't you? Those nice people living near here and—and their children. There's a daughter away from home, isn't there? The eldest, I suppose—she sounded delightful. Is she pretty?'

He looked at her with mild astonishment. 'Very pretty and utterly charming. Shall we keep to the point, Celine?'

She gulped. 'Yes—I'm sorry. You see, I feel awkward. I know that's silly, because we never were engaged, were we? So there's no reason why ...' If she went on much longer she was going to burst into tears. 'Please take me home,' she begged him in a voice rigid with control.

Oliver got up at once. 'Perhaps that would be best, there's not much point in talking at present, is there?' He gave her a gentle smile and she held on to a table, otherwise she would have flung herself at him and made a fearful exhibition of herself, weeping and wailing all over him. Thinking about it afterwards, she found she couldn't remember much of the drive back. Oliver had talked calmly of this and that, seen her into the surgery, wished her a friendly goodnight and driven away again.

She never wore her ring while she was working, so there was no need to explain anything to Maggie; she would know soon enough. Celine went about her day's work much as usual, unaware that her pale strained face was giving Maggie a good deal of thought. It became even paler when Oliver arrived in the afternoon, but she didn't falter in her various duties and answered him in a normal if slightly wooden voice when he spoke to her. And that was seldom. And before he left he called Maggie into the office and that lady came out presently looking bewildered, although she burst at once into brisk demands for Celine to do this and that and the other thing. It was only much later, when she was on the point of going home, that she said gruffly: 'Sorry to hear you're leaving us, Celine—quite a shock, I can tell you. But I suppose it's better to find out that you're not suited before you marry, although I could have bet my bottom dollar that you were an ideal couple. I'm really sorry, my dear. Dr Seymour says there are one or two girls coming tomorrow to be interviewed for your job.'

Celine's face felt stiff, but she managed some kind of a smile. Oliver hadn't wasted a moment, he must have been impatient for her to go. After all, the eldest daughter would be coming home any day now . . .

Four girls came for an interview and Oliver saw them all. Afterwards he told Maggie that one of them seemed very suitable, what was more to the point, she was anxious to begin work as soon as possible. In two days' time, in fact, he added. And perhaps Maggie would be good enough to let Celine know.

Celine packed, did two days' work with comendable efficiency, relieved that there was no sign of Oliver, and spent the last afternoon showing her successor the ropes. She was a nice girl, small and dark and dainty, and she made Celine feel like a giantess. It was obvious from the start that she was going to be far better at the job than Celine had ever been.

She still hadn't seen Oliver, but he would be taking the clinic in the morning. She went down as usual and worked with the new girl, then went to say goodbye to Maggie and Nurse Byng. Dorothy, back from sick leave, was stunned by the news and broke into a great many unfinished sentences which Maggie ruthlessly cut short. 'We're very sorry,' she said brusquely. 'Heaven knows where Dr Seymour will find another girl like you.'

'Well, there's that eldest daughter of those friends of his,' said Celine, turning the knife in the wound.

Maggie turned astonished eyes on her. 'Her? The child's barely thirteen—there's been a joke going round about her marrying him since she could toddle—he's her godfather, I believe.' She paused. 'Do you feel all right, Celine? You've gone very pale.'

'I'm fine.' Celine took a calming breath. 'I must see Dr Seymour when he comes . . .'

'Well, he's here now,' said Dorothy, and pulled her colleague into the first aid room, where, much against her inclination, she shut the door.

He looked tired and vaguely unapproachable, but Celine didn't heed that. She began the moment he set foot inside the door. 'Oliver, I must speak to you.'

He barely glanced at her. 'Not now, Celine.' He gave her a faintly mocking smile. 'You know where to find me if you want me.'

She watched him go into the office and pick up the phone and start talking urgently. It would be no good, she could see that; what she wanted to say required his undivided attention.

She supposed he didn't intend to say goodbye, but when presently she went downstairs with her bags she found David waiting for her.

'I'll take you to the station,' he told her. 'Dr Seymour is waiting for a phone call. He'll be out in a second.'

It couldn't have been a more public place in which to say goodbye. Under the interested eyes of a dozen or more mothers and children, Celine offered a hand and felt Oliver's engulf it, but there was no chance to say much other than goodbye. That didn't really matter, because she had heard him telling David that he would be at home and could be reached there.

She searched Oliver's face as she shook hands, but there was nothing there to comfort her, only a pleasant smile tinged with a touch of impatience because she was holding up the clinic. She got into the car with David and didn't look back.

At the station she prevailed upon him to leave her at the ticket office. 'There's plenty of time before my train goes,' she told him, 'and I know how busy you are this morning.' She waved gaily as he got back into the car and the moment he had gone put her case in the left luggage office and went to find a taxi. It took quite some time to get to Strand on the Green, but it didn't matter; the clinic would have finished and Oliver would be home by now. Celine paid off the taxi and rang the door bell.

Pym's welcoming smile made it evident that they didn't know she was going home. He invited her in, but when she asked to see Oliver he shook his head. 'The doctor rang not ten minutes ago,' he told her. 'He's off to Birmingham, miss—didn't say when he'd be back. Would you like to leave a message, though I daresay he'll be in touch with you. In rather a hurry, I gather.'

She had been so sure of seeing him that she didn't quite believe it. She looked at Pym from eyes suddenly filled with tears. 'No, it doesn't matter, Pym,' she said incoherently. 'Sometimes things aren't meant to happen, are they, however much you want them to.'

He looked at her anxiously. 'You must sit down, Miss Baylis. I'll get Mrs Pym to make you a nice cup of tea.'

She shook her head. 'No, thank you, Pym. It's very good of you, but I'll go.' She stood up. 'Don't tell the doctor I've called.' She quite forgot that he didn't know about the whole sorry business. 'We said goodbye this morning—it was just something . . . it doesn't matter now.'

Pym was discreet and he liked her. He and Mrs Pym had decided the first time they had set eyes on her that she was the one for the doctor. All he said was: 'Very well, miss. I'll call a taxi.'

She was getting into it when she was hailed from the pavement—Mrs Weatherby, with a pretty girl beside her. 'Hullo there,' she cried cheerfully. 'Did you have a heavenly time in Holland? I suppose Oliver's up to his neck in work again.' She smiled cosily at Celine. 'Here's our daughter Hilary—I told her Oliver was going to marry you and she hopes you'll have her for a bridesmaid; she's decided he's too old for her!' She laughed and her daughter laughed with her. She was exactly as Oliver had said; very pretty and utterly charming and not a day over fourteen.

Celine made a great effort. 'We'll have to get together about that. Now I simply must fly . . .'

'Ah, going to meet Oliver, I expect. See you soon, my dear.'

They stood and waved from the pavement and she waved back, quite unable to see them through her tears.

She had dried them by the time they reached the

station. She caught the next train, although it stopped all over the place and took hours. It was lovely to be going home, but she was dreading it all the same.

Dusty saw her first as she got out of the village taxi in front of the open door. He shambled out to meet her, barking loudly and knocking things over in his excitement, and then her mother came, and her father. Mercifully there were people staying the night and Aunt Chloe was fully occupied, so Celine was able to go to her father's study and explain—if her mumbled disjointed account could be called an explanation. She hadn't made it very clear, but even if they didn't understand they knew what to do. Her father gave her a glass of his best brandy, her mother went in search of Barney and Angela, gave Aunt Chloe a brief résumé of what was happening and went back to the study. 'You've had a nasty day, darling,' she declared. 'You're going to bed, and Angela's making you a lovely meal and you'll have it there. You're not to worry about a thing, and in the morning we'll sit down quietly and talk everything over.'

And Celine was glad to do as she was told.

In all the books she had read, the heroine always spent long nights tossing and turning in bed, weeping buckets. Celine expected to do the same, so she was very surprised to wake up very early the next morning, with the vague remembrance of dozing off over her supper. She sat up in bed and looked around her familiar room. Someone had unpacked her things, taken away the supper tray and pulled the curtains together. She got up now and drew them back. It was a perfect morning, still with a faint pearly chill. There were birds singing and the sound of a tractor far off, not at all like Bethnal Green. She closed her eyes on the thought and started to dress. A Liberty cotton which had seen better days but was still nonetheless charming, and her hair brushed out and left as it was, and never mind the make-up. She crept silently through the old house and down to the kitchen where she made tea, hushed Dusty, and then went out into the garden.

She made for the swing; she had always gone there to think about things, to worry, or dream. She sailed gently to and fro, Dusty sitting happily beside her, and looked around her. It had been a splendid summer, she reflected, the garden was at its best and the house glowed warm in the rising sun. 'It isn't so long ago that we were here, doing just this,' she told Dusty, 'and think of all the things that have happened since then—and oh, Dusty dear, I wish none of them had—at least, I think so, only then I wouldn't have met Oliver, but if I hadn't met him I wouldn't be unhappy now, would I?'

Dusty made a sympathetic snorting noise and then pricked his ears and sat up. 'The milkman,' said Celine. 'He's early, you can lie down again.'

But Dusty got to his feet as racing round the corner of the house came two Jack Russells and behind them came Oliver.

Celine stopped swinging and he crossed the grass and stood in front of her.

'I'm told you wanted to see me,' he said very quietly.

Celine stared up at him; she wasn't to know that Pym, upset by the tears, had consulted Mrs Pym, who had told him to ring the doctor without delay.

'Depend upon it,' she had said, 'the path of true love never did run smooth.'

She said at last, 'You must have left London very early.'

'Two o'clock this morning.'

He looked tired, although he was freshly shaven and he still contrived to be elegant. 'Well?' he said, and she knew from the tone of his voice that she would have to answer him.

It was difficult to know where to start. She went on staring, her mouth open, trying to find the words. She was holding the ropes of the swing and Oliver put his hands over hers, and she found that reassuring. All the same, she began at the wrong end: 'Hilary's just as you said, very pretty and utterly charming, but she's about fourteen. I didn't know that.'

It took him fifteen seconds to work that one out. 'I've been in love with you since we met,' he told her softly, 'and I've loved you a little more each day. When did you discover that you loved me?'

'You were sitting on the stairs reading the paper, only I think I've loved you all the time too, but I thought you were just being kind, and then I was told about this girl—I didn't know she was still at school, and I wanted to tell you, but you said not now.'

A tear trickled down one cheek, but he wiped it away with a finger.

'When I kissed you in Theo's garden you pulled away from me. Why?'

'I was so afraid you'd guess ...' She smiled at him, and he lifted her off the swing and wrapped his arms around her. He kissed her for quite some time, watched by the three dogs, her mother, who had heard the car and had got up to look out of the bedroom window, and Barney, who liked to begin his days early.

'They do say,' said Barney to no one in particular, 'as how it's love as makes the world go round, and by golly, it must be fair whizzing.'

But however fast the world was spinning, time was standing still for Celine and Oliver, held in a magic moment they would never forget.